——————— ★

Approaching along the water's edge, I became curious. That wasn't driftwood. The next time the wave washed out, I crossed the wet sand for a better look. And wished I hadn't. So this was where Devin Ballantine had disappeared to. If only someone else had found the missing Casanova.

I screamed for help and a number of people leaned over the pier's railing to ask what was wrong. I pointed and stammered and cried, "There! There!" When I pulled my cell phone out of my pocket and dialed 9-1-1, I was so choked up I could hardly speak.

——————— ★ ———————

Previously published Worldwide Mystery titles by
ELLEN ELIZABETH HUNTER

MURDER ON THE CANDLELIGHT TOUR
MURDER AT THE AZALEA FESTIVAL

MURDER AT WRIGHTSVILLE BEACH

Ellen Elizabeth Hunter

W🌐RLDWIDE®

TORONTO • NEW YORK • LONDON
AMSTERDAM • PARIS • SYDNEY • HAMBURG
STOCKHOLM • ATHENS • TOKYO • MILAN
MADRID • WARSAW • BUDAPEST • AUCKLAND

Recycling programs
for this product may
not exist in your area.

MURDER AT WRIGHTSVILLE BEACH

A Worldwide Mystery/March 2009

First published by Magnolia Mysteries.

ISBN-13: 978-0-373-26667-8
ISBN-10:   0-373-26667-7

Printed in U.S.A.

Acknowledgments

Dear Reader,

Researching this book was a delightful culinary, shopping, and vacationing experience. Sampling our delicious coastal food, shopping at Lumina Station, exploring Wrightsville Beach and Carolina Heights: true treats, every one.

For background on the POW experience in North Carolina, I read articles by Tom Belton, Curator of Military History at the NC Museum of History, and Wilbur D. Jones, Jr.'s *Sentimental Journey: Memoirs of a Wartime Boomtown.*

Keep in mind that Valentine's Art Gallery is a fictional place, so is the shag club on the Causeway: if only it were real. Bella Aqua, Melanie's rental "cottage" is a composite of the beach houses I've stayed in. The Lauder family's 1920s Georgian Revival house was inspired by a house I once owned: my favorite. You can see a picture of it on my website, www.ellenhunter.com.

All the other wonderful places I've described are real and await your visit. I've had my fun, it's your turn. So drag out that beach chair, put up the beach umbrella, prop up your feet, and enjoy.

With warmest regards,
Ellen

ONE

ON FRIDAY AFTERNOON we stepped out of the heat and sunlight into the cool, shadowy interior of Valentine's Art Gallery. "Hey girlfriend, I brought you some customers!" I called as I quickly shoved the door shut behind me before Val could bellow: Don't let the hot air in!

But Valentine seemed not to notice. Seated in her favorite black leather wing chair behind the reflective expanse of a glass-topped table desk, she stared fixedly at the view outside the plate glass windows.

Valentine Russo was a large, bossy woman with an abundance of attitude and springy jet black hair that she wore loose and flowing. She favored denim skirts, Oxford cloth shirts, and silver jewelry by the yard. I knew her as a tireless volunteer of Turtle Watch, an environmental group where I help out. We had joined forces on many occasions to protect loggerhead turtle nests and hatchlings from predators that included the two-legged variety.

Valentine's Art Gallery and Valentine herself

were permanent fixtures in the small coastal community of Wrightsville Beach. Kind-hearted and generous to a fault, Val had provided encouragement and gallery wall space to emerging talent for decades. For those reasons I respected her and sent my clients to her when they were shopping for the Van Goghs of tomorrow. Valentine's instinct for talent was unerring.

I am Ashley Wilkes, a historic preservationist. My partner Jon Campbell and I restore old houses in the Greater Wilmington area. It was August and for the next few weeks until after Labor Day I would be staying at Wrightsville Beach. My sister Melanie who is a successful realtor had rented an oceanfront sleeps-14 "cottage" for the season. I had a suite all to myself.

After a light lunch on Melanie's top deck with its fabulous view of the green Atlantic (today it was green; only God knew what color He'd paint it tomorrow), she, I, and her houseguest super-model Kelly Lauder headed to Valentine's.

"Why is Val ignoring us?" Melanie asked, the irritation in her voice an indication that she was miffed by Valentine's failure to welcome paying customers with Southern hospitality plus an appropriate dose of entrepreneurial groveling.

Valentine remained as posed and unresponsive

as any of the portraits she had ever exhibited on the gallery's dove gray walls. I turned to look where she was staring but saw nothing unusual: the sun reflecting off the concrete expanse of Johnnie Mercer's pier, the waves of heat dancing on the sand like dervishes on hot coals.

I shrugged. "I don't know. Valentine is a power unto herself. She'll say hello when she's good and ready."

The gallery felt cold and the ceiling spotlights had been extinguished, a welcome relief from ninety degree temperatures and the glare of sun and sand. Ambient daylight slanted through the windows creating stripes of pale yellow and gray across the walls and floor.

Kelly, in short-shorts and a tank top, sauntered to the center of the room, her flipflops slapping the pale oak floor. Hands on hips, she demanded, "Where's Uncle J.C.'s new painting? It's supposed to be here."

Kelly was right. J.C. Lauder's latest painting was not hanging as promised in the brochure and as described to us by Val herself in a telephone invitation that morning. A reception was scheduled for four p.m. but she had invited us for a private preview. Neither were there any other pictures, even though I picked out the tiny shadows of hooks. The walls were bare.

Only two days earlier I had bought one of J.C. Lauder's watercolors from Val. It was small but evocative of the Victorian era, a charming depiction of an ancient, leaning gazebo covered with vines. Perfect for my Victorian library where I'd immediately taken it and hung it.

I looked around the room, confused, then turned to Valentine for an explanation. "Val…?"

But Valentine remained inscrutable. She did not rise to greet us, nor did she boom her customary, "Hey gal!" In fact, she hadn't moved at all. "She looks…"

"Strange, even for her," Melanie said, hurrying over to the desk where a brass lamp with a black shade glowed softly. The heels of her slides tapped the hardwood floor. She had on capri pants and a cropped top that rode up her midriff as she leaned across the glass to confront Valentine. "Say something, Valentine. What's wrong with you?" She turned to me, a troubled expression vexing her pretty face. "Something's wrong with her. She's in some kind of trance."

"Something's definitely wrong. I think she's…"

Kelly closed the distance, snapped her fingers in Valentine's face and pronounced, "She's stoned!"

But Valentine did not do drugs. On closer inspection, she looked ghastly. Her unblinking gaze remained riveted on some illusive something outside the windows. Her flyaway hair fell across her forehead, concealing one cheek. I saw her hands then, clutching the armrests, fingers curled and rigid, as spastic as claws.

"Why is it so cold in here?" Melanie complained and straightened up to rub her arms.

"I think we'd better call 911," I said. "I think she's had a stroke." I scurried around the glass tabletop to Valentine's side and gently touched her arm. Her skin was cold to the touch in the air-conditioned air. I gave her arm a gentle shake. "Val?"

She slipped sideways, the wing of the chair catching her sliding head. An unruly strand of dark hair fell away, exposing her forehead.

Melanie shrieked, "Oh my God!"

A glistening glob like a dab of wet black paint dotted the olive skin on her forehead. I swallowed air and held it in my lungs. I knew that if I looked at the back of her head it would be a mess. I didn't look. "She's…"

"Oh my God, not dead," Melanie cried.

"…been shot," I finished lamely.

"And robbed," Kelly added.

"JEEZ, WHY WOULD ANYONE want to shoot Val Russo?" asked the first cop on the scene. He was about my age, twenty-five or twenty-six, and looked hot and tired and like he'd like to get into shorts and a tank top himself instead of the buttoned-up uniform he was wearing. On second thought, from the devouring looks he was casting in Kelly's direction, it was her shorts and tank top he wanted to get into. But he was a professional and realized he was on duty and this was no ordinary call, still his eyes darted back and forth between the victim and the super model. I sighed heavily. The attention showered on Kelly by every male who came within a mile of her was becoming annoying.

"Aren't you…?" the officer asked.

"Yes," she replied with petulant impatience and did one of those slinky runway walks around the gallery, keeping a distance between herself and Val.

The cop had put on his hat when he got out of the Wrightsville PD cruiser but now he took it off, thought better of setting it down on Valentine's desk, and just held it in his hand.

"What are you waiting for?" Melanie exploded. "Do something!"

He turned to her. You could see it in his eyes: Wow, two knockouts in one room! He looked at me. Not bad either. "I've secured the scene," he replied, "and we're waiting for the M.E. Val is dead but only the doc can pronounce. And the investigators are on their way."

The Wrightsville Police Department is located next to Town Hall on the Causeway on Harbour Island, a two-minute drive away. One minute if they had the sirens blaring.

He chatted nervously, "Val Russo was good to everyone on this island, even the surfers. The artists loved her. She gave them all a chance, even the bad ones." He looked toward the rear of the gallery, to a short hallway that led to an alley. "She even let the kids set up a ramp for their skateboards out there. Then gave them money for ice cream. Who'd want to kill a nice lady like that?"

I noticed he'd stopped looking at her. It was disconcerting having her sitting there behind the desk like that, watching the scene outside. She was there, but not there.

"The motive was robbery," Kelly said flatly from across the room. "My uncle's new painting was here. Someone stole it. And all the other pictures."

For some reason the cop looked to me for verification. "That true?"

"Yes," I replied, and reached for a brochure from atop the stack on the corner of Val's desk.

His hand stopped me and I was surprised at how fast he moved. "Don't touch anything!"

"Sorry," I said. Married to Wilmington PD Lieutenant Nick Yost, I knew better.

"What's this missing painting worth?" he wanted to know.

Kelly replied, "Nobody knows. Not yet. Besides it wasn't for sale. Uncle J.C. was doing Miss Russo a favor by letting her exhibit it because she had helped him out in the early days. The painting, all his paintings, are being shipped to New York in a couple of weeks. There's going to be a big auction at Christie's right after Labor Day."

Outside the window, police cars and an ambulance roared up to the gallery, all at once, all together. They parked every which way. Law enforcement types got out including a short woman with a medical bag, and another woman whom I recognized immediately: Diane Sherwood, homicide detective for Wilmington PD. She was dressed in beach clothes like us, shorts and a tee shirt. But she was outside her jurisdiction. What was she doing here? On vacation? A friend of the doctor's?

Instantly the gallery was filled to overflowing with detectives. The Chief must have sent the whole team. How often did peaceful, quiet, family-style Wrightsville Beach get a homicide? Probably almost never. This was a place where families vacationed, where people bicycled and rollerbladed and went out for fish suppers. Where the sun shone and the sky was always Carolina Blue. Bad things did not happen at Wrightsville Beach.

Melanie, Kelly, and I were herded into a corner. Diane Sherwood flicked a cool eye over us and strolled over. "Don't tell me," she said. "You found the body. Nick is right. You are a magnet for murder!"

TWO

THE POLICE MOVED US outside to a bench in front of the gallery while a forensics photographer took pictures of the "crime scene" and the doctor examined Val's body. I still couldn't believe that she was dead. "Why would someone shoot Valentine Russo?" I asked, echoing the police officer.

"Well, obviously, someone wanted Uncle J.C.'s latest painting bad enough to kill for it," Kelly pronounced.

"You know, Kelly, I've been thinking about that and it just doesn't make sense. Okay, so somebody wanted J.C.'s painting, but then why take all the other paintings? From the descriptions in the brochure, they were works of art by unknowns. Why would someone steal them? They could be purchased for about a hundred bucks a piece."

"People kill wantonly these days for the most insignificant reasons," Melanie said, fanning her face with her hand. "The politicians have made it too easy to get a gun."

Melanie sells really expensive coastal properties. She's been voted Wilmington's top realtor time
and time again and I am so proud of her. She's older
than me by eight years, thirty-four to my twenty-
six.

Our mother, Claire Wilkes, had named us
Melanie and Ashley. Mama had always been
besotted with *Gone With the Wind*. I've often
wondered if his name was what initially attracted
her to Daddy, the late Judge Peter Wilkes. But then
she'd fallen madly in love with him, for what
woman could resist my darling father with his
courtly, Old South manners. Melanie and I have
often joked that it was a good thing we didn't have
a brother, for surely Mama would have named him
Rhett Butler Wilkes!

For sisters we're as different as night and day and
there's no familial resemblance between us.
Melanie favors our mother, Claire Chastain Wilkes,
with her creamy complexion and vibrant auburn
hair, eyes that are intensely green and gold. I take
after Daddy, Peter Wilkes, having inherited his
delicate heart-shaped face, and eyes that are so
deeply blue-gray they sometimes appear violet. I've
also got his abundant dark hair that curls tena-
ciously in our humid climate.

The police cars had attracted a crowd. Then the

curiosity seekers spotted Kelly and went wild. If it were not for the police barricade and the officers assigned to secure the perimeter, we would have been mobbed.

Kelly's picture was often featured on the covers of *People* and *Town & Country*, *Vogue* and *Harper's Bazaar*. Her mother Babe Lauder had been a top model in the sixties. Kelly used the Lauder name although she was Ted Douglas's daughter. Like Babe, Kelly was a natural blonde with hair so pale it was platinum. Her eyes were big and china blue, and her skin was very fair. She withdrew a tube of sun block from her straw tote bag and began rubbing cream on her arms.

Although Babe and Ted lived in New York, Kelly had spent her high school years in Wilmington, staying with the Lauder patriarch, Joseph Lauder, at the Lauder family home-place on Grace Street. She and Melanie had been best friends in high school and have remained best friends ever since.

I watched idly as two additional patrol cars pulled up and parked crosswise on Lumina Avenue, closing off the street. The officers got out and shepherded the crowd away from the gallery.

"Well, then," I said, continuing our argument about the crime, "if Val was killed because she was trying to prevent a robbery, why was she sitting at her desk? If she had tried to thwart a robber, there would have been signs of a struggle, things would have been knocked over, and we would have found her lying on the floor, not sitting there behind her desk as if she had been having a conversation."

"Ashley's got a point," Melanie told Kelly. "And Ashley has lots of experience with homicides. She's been involved in homicide cases in the past. And married to a police lieutenant the way she is, she knows a lot about police procedure."

This wasn't true but I didn't feel like challenging the point.

"When am I going to meet Nick?" Kelly asked. "Is he coming home for the weekend?"

"I hope so," I replied.

"Have you heard from him, shug?" Melanie asked gently.

She knew how worried I was about Nick. "Uh, not yet." I'd been leaving messages for my husband on his cell phone for days and he had not called back, and I was very worried.

"I'd better call him now, before he hears of Val's murder and my involvement from someone else," I said, digging my cell phone out of my purse. Nick hates it when I get too close to a homicide case. And wouldn't Diane Sherwood love to be the one to break the news to him?

As I listened to his voice mail message, I watched a throng of onlookers migrate up the ramp to Johnnie Mercer's pier for a better view. Almost ten years ago the landmark pier had been destroyed by two hurricanes. The entire pier, including the pilings, had been rebuilt in concrete. You either loved it or you hated it. I missed the old wooden pier but understood why it had to be rebuilt to withstand storms.

"Nick, it's me Ashley. Listen, something has happened here and I've got to talk to you right away. So call me as soon as you get this message. Love you." I tapped the end button.

Diane Sherwood came out of the gallery and stood over the three of us as we sat on the bench. "Did you know her well?" she asked.

"I did," I replied. "She was a good person, very popular with the residents and tourists alike. I can't imagine anyone shooting her. Was it a robbery?"

"The paintings that were supposed to be on exhibit are not anywhere inside so it might have been a robbery," Diane said, not telling us anything we had not already surmised for ourselves.

"I told you so," Kelly declared.

"Officer Meriweather is coming out to record your statements, then you can go. That's what I came to tell you." Looking at Kelly, she said, "You're not planning to return to New York soon, are you?"

"No, I'll be staying with Melanie for a while. I've hired Ashley to restore my family's house in Carolina Heights, so I'll be around to help her get started. Why? Am I forbidden to leave? If that's the case, I'm calling my lawyer right now. You can't hold me here. I had nothing to do with that… that…" She pointed to the gallery.

Diane drew herself up. Every other time I'd seen her in the past she'd been wearing mannish pant-suits with boxy jackets that concealed a gun. Today, even in shorts and a camp shirt, she looked tailored. No sign of a weapon. And she had on sensible boat shoes, not the flip flops most women wear at the beach. "Take it easy, Miss Lauder. No one's holding you. We'd just like to get your statement and we want to know where to reach you." She lifted her chestnut hair off the back of her neck. "Sure is hot. I'd better get back inside."

"Aren't you out of your jurisdiction?" I asked.

"I'm staying with Sarah," she replied. "The M.E. We're…friends."

Then she turned and said to me as if an after-thought, "What do you hear from Nick, Ashley?"

Diane and Nick had worked together on homicide cases for Wilmington PD before he was assigned to Homeland Security.

"He's busy," I said, feeling defensive. I didn't

want this woman to know that my husband was not returning my calls or that I had not heard from him in five days.

"Well, you've got to admire him," Diane continued, "the way he devoted his spare time for the past year to those intensive courses in Arabic…"

"He's got a gift for languages," I bragged.

"Then being recruited to translate 'chatter' for the CIA. Lots of guys on the force wish they were in his shoes, I can tell you that. Where the action is."

Where the action is, but not where his wife is, I thought resentfully. And was Diane Sherwood one of the "guys" who wished she was working for Homeland Security, rounding up terrorists instead of rounding up punk drug dealers?

She said again, "I've got to get inside. They asked me to lend a hand. Officer Meriweather will be right out." A stream of cool air flowed out from the gallery as she passed through the door.

"Oh, look, it's Jon," Melanie cried, pointing to a figure the police were letting through.

Thank God, a friendly face, I thought. Jon, my partner, my best friend. The sight of him—his golden hair, his ruddy complexion, his concerned expression—was such a comfort. "Jon, how did you get through?" I asked.

"I'm a permanent resident, remember? I know all the guys on the force."

Jon lives on the north end of the island in a salmon pink stucco house that backs up to the marshes. "But they wouldn't tell me what's going on, only that there's been a crime."

Before I could respond, Kelly stood up and stuck out her hand. "Hi, I'm Kelly Lauder." What she was really saying was: Look at me! Surely you know I'm a famous super model. Surely you can see that my long mane is pale blonde, that my legs are long and sleek, that my bust is high and full.

"Oh, hi," Jon said casually. "I heard you were visiting Melanie. You may not remember me but we were in Biology class together."

"Of course I remember you, Jon. How could I forget you?"

How indeed? I wanted to say. Kelly seemed to need attention from men the way other women needed air. This egotistical Barbie doll was starting to get on my nerves.

I nipped this little flirtation in the bud. "Val's been murdered, Jon," I cried, and got his full attention. "She was shot in the forehead." I went on to give him a quick sketch of what had happened.

THREE

OFFICER MERIWEATHER INTRODUCED himself and taped our statements on a tape recorder. After instructing us to come to the station tomorrow to sign a typescript of them, he let us go. Jon rode back to the house with us in Melanie's Jaguar, the police clearing a lane for our departure.

She whipped down Lumina Avenue toward the bridge. Melanie has only two speeds when behind the wheel: stop and fast. She could wallpaper a room with her speeding citations. At the bridge she picked up Waynick Boulevard where she pulled into the left lane and shot past a driver who was doing the speed limit. All the cops were back at Valentine's, she must have reasoned, so who was there to ticket her when she floored the accelerator? No one.

Out on Banks Channel there wasn't a hint of a breeze to ruffle the placid water. Yachts lay at anchor lethargically as if defeated by the heat. A few sailboats floated lazily, their sails becalmed.

Across the channel, two and three story beach houses crowded the shores of Harbour Island. In the background, the Seapath Towers rose starkly white against the dark green horizon that delineated the mainland.

In the back seat with Jon I filled him in on the details of our finding Valentine and told him that all the paintings were missing. "I know they were there this morning," I said. "Valentine telephoned to invite us for a private preview before the reception."

Kelly turned around and repeated her theory that someone had stolen her uncle's painting and had shot Valentine because she was in the way.

"I got an invitation to that exhibit," Jon commented. "It was scheduled for four. I was planning to attend later. Everyone here admires your uncle's work."

"Well now no one will be able to see his latest painting and Valentine told me she thought it was his best," Kelly said.

"Didn't you ever see it?" I asked.

"No," she pouted. "He was keeping it a secret until the unveiling."

"Shouldn't you call him and tell him it's missing?" I asked.

"Let the police do that," Kelly responded. "I

don't want to be the one to break bad news to Uncle J.C. You must not know anything about him if you don't know that."

"Well, shut my mouth," I murmured to Jon.

In the front seat, Melanie and Kelly were re-counting how Valentine had looked, then without warning they switched to the cookout they were planning for tonight.

"Stay for dinner, Jon," Melanie called, and turned her head for his reply.

"Watch the road," I shouted, as I frequently do when riding with Melanie.

Idly, I listened to their chatter. "And I've got a hottie for you, hon," Melanie told Kelly. Then the talk switched to recipes. It seemed that in addition to all her other virtues Kelly was a top notch cook; she'd studied at elite cooking schools. I can barely boil water. I tuned them out. I still couldn't believe that Valentine was gone. She had been beloved by the community, just as the cop had said. No husband, no children. No enemies. The permanent residents of Wrightsville Beach were her extended family, the artists were her children. She spent more time in the gallery than in her home.

"Jon, you live out here year round, did Valentine have a quarrel with anyone?"

He shook his golden head negatively. "Valentine's heart was as big as everything else about her. Very popular, invited to every party, sat on just about every committee. That gallery was her life. Oh, I did hear gossip that Gordon Cushman objected when she raised her prices but she just told him to go buy his paintings somewhere else, said she was personally committed to putting a stop to the 'starving artist' syndrome and would see to it that they got paid what they deserved."

"Sounds like our Valentine," I commented with admiration. I *had* admired Valentine, I mused, she was unique, a one-of-a-kind personality. In a small community like this, she would be missed.

So Gordon Cushman had had a dispute with Valentine. Cushman, not one of my favorite people, had been married to true-crime writer Cecily Cushman, now deceased. He'd lived off her earnings for all of their married life and fancied himself an art collector and connoisseur.

"Are you talking about poor Gordon?" Melanie called. "That poor man is having serious financial problems. We all thought Cecily left him a bundle but she didn't."

"And you know this how?" I asked.

Melanie turned to me.

"Watch the road!" I yelled.

"I make it my business to know who might be

selling and who might be buying. How do you think I get so many listings?" She turned her attention back to her driving and I let out my breath. "Wonder what the Cushmans did with all the money Cecily made? Her books were made into movies. You know that's the big bucks.

"There used to be a saying in Wilmington: 'There's Confederate money, and then there's old money.' Well, now there's a lot of new money in town and I aim to get a slice of it. A large slice. Anyway, I invited Gordon over for coffee and dessert later tonight."

Kelly said, "I bought all the ingredients for *tiramisu* yesterday," and launched into a recitation of the recipe, along with a description of the one and only particular brand of lady fingers she was willing to use.

Melanie picked up the southern leg of Lumina Avenue and followed it to the south end of the island. We pulled into a paved driveway in front of *Bella Aqua*, her rental house. At Wrightsville Beach, all the houses have names. *Bella Aqua* was three stories tall if you counted the enclosure under the house. The ground level housed a garage and storage rooms, an area that could withstand flooding without experiencing too much damage if sea water flowed through the pilings when there was storm surge as frequently happened during hurricane season.

The house was sand color with a lot of painted white trim. Decks and balconies and little porches covered the front and back sides of the house. From the ocean-side decks one had spectacular views of the "beautiful water" for which the house had been named.

A black Ford Bronco was parked on the pavement. Uh oh, Mickey Ballantine. "Bad News" Ballantine as I called him to myself. I suspected Mickey was guilty of a lot of unsavory activities—running a chop shop for stolen cars was high on the list. Melanie has a thing for bad boys. The more dangerous they are, the more they get her juices bubbling.

We headed up a flight of outside stairs to a little covered porch. When Melanie pushed the door open into a short hallway, Spunky was instantly there, wrapping his furry body around her ankles and wailing a long plaintive meow. Spunky does not like Mickey. Animals have better sense than people about who is worth knowing and who is not.

Spunky is a cat I rescued one cold December when he was a tiny kitten. As soon as he was old enough to develop discernment, he took one look into Melanie's yellow-green kittenish eyes and found a kindred spirit. He howled when she left my house. He behaved absolutely pitifully, went off his food, sulked. I had no choice but to give Spunky to

Melanie. He adores her and follows her around like a puppy-dog. And she is very, very good to him. Black with a white bib and paws, he looks like a plump, satisfied feline in a tuxedo. So far he had not been tempted to venture out of doors, not even onto the deck.

Melanie scooped him up in her arms and the volume of his purr escalated to motorboat level. "Mickey's here. Did you say hello to Mickey?" Melanie purred back, burying her face in his fur.

He narrowed his eyes and twitched his tail as if annoyed, evidently not liking the sound of Mickey's name on his mistress's lips.

A flight of enclosed stairs led to the top floor where a vaulted-ceilinged greatroom was flooded with light from windows on three sides. Most of the top floor was one huge open space housing a kitchen, dining area, and sitting area with a plasma TV. Topside, we called it. The master bedroom suite was on this level too, the guest rooms down on the middle level. A massive pool table dominated a corner of the great-room.

Mickey was shooting pool with another man who looked like a younger version of himself. Aha! So this was the hottie Melanie had referred to, intended as boy-toy entertainment for Kelly, no doubt. Mickey leaned the cue stick against the table and growled, "Hey, babe," to Melanie and opened his arms. She walked into them to receive his kiss.

"Put the cat down, babe," Mickey said, not at all friendly.

Melanie lowered Spunky to the floor, then Mickey took her in his arms and kissed her so intimately it was embarrassing to watch. Right before I turned away, the other man winked at me. The hair on the back of my neck prickled. Beware, my instincts warned.

Kelly seemed not to notice. She was doing her "Hey, look at me!" routine. She introduced herself to the other man and I heard him say he was Mickey's brother, Devin. And that explained the heap of luggage piled up against the white wall near the stairs.

The house should have been named *Bella Blanc*—everything was white. The walls were white and the carpeting, the sectional furniture, the shades and draperies. There was not a spot of color in the decor, not a single picture on the walls. They were white and stark and the only relief to all this whiteness was a great expanse of glass that framed sky, sand, and ocean.

By contrast, the pool table was an inviting oasis of green felt and gleaming mahogany on massive Chippendale-style legs to which everyone seemed to gravitate.

Melanie caught her breath and introduced us all to each other. Mickey still had his arm wrapped around her waist and they looked like they wanted to be alone. I suspected that shortly they would adjourn to the bedroom and, sure enough, within minutes, Mickey was picking up his luggage and Melanie said she was going to help him unpack. Uh huh!

"Show Devin to one of the guest rooms, will you, shug?" she called over her shoulder as she trailed slavishly after Mickey. Spunky followed her with the same groveling show of adoration that she was showering on Mickey. *Oh, Melanie!*

I went to the refrigerator and pulled out a jug of iced tea—first things first—and filled four tall glasses.

Jon started telling Devin that there'd been a murder on the island and that we'd found the victim, while Kelly sat on the sectional, crossing and uncrossing her legs and examining her cuticles. Devin asked a surprising amount of questions about Valentine and the gallery in a manner that reminded me of the method Nick used when asking questions. *Oh, Nick, I miss you.*

Seeing that the men were ignoring her with their recitation of crime wave statistics, Kelly got up and announced, "I'm going to my room to take an aspirin and lie down. This has been a gruesome day."

"So, Devin Ballantine, how long are you staying?" I asked after she sauntered to the stairs. I refilled our glasses at the center island.

"Ummm, not sure. A week, maybe two. Depends."

"Depends on what?" Jon asked.

"How long it takes to find a boat. That's why I'm down here, I'm buying a boat."

"That shouldn't take long," Jon said, and I got the impression he wasn't too keen on having Devin hang around for very long. He kind of rubbed me the wrong way too—overly confident, smug, self-satisfied, good looking and he knew it.

Be fair, Ashley, I told myself. You've only just met him. Yes, and he's got one strike against him from the get-go—he's Mickey's brother. "Let me show you to your room," I told him. "Jon, you're staying for dinner, aren't you? I think I'm going to take a nap too. I've got a suite and there's a sofa in the sitting room if you want to stretch out."

I glanced in the direction of the master bedroom. Spunky sat outside the closed door as still as a statue, listening intently to sounds I could not hear. Was grateful I could not hear. You won't be seeing her for hours, I wanted to tell him.

I picked him up and took him with me as I led the way down the enclosed staircase. Jon grabbed one suitcase, Devin the other and they followed me. As I reached past Devin to open the door to his room, I caught a strong whiff of musk oil. Too powerful, too cloying.

About fifteen minutes later our little household had settled down for a *siesta*.

FOUR

WE WERE OUT ON the top deck enjoying the sunset. From up here we had a spectacular view of the ocean. Yet by leaning over the side railing one also had a view of the west where the ICW was swallowing the sun. Golden rays slanted across the narrow island, shimmered on the waves and set the ocean ablaze with color. Devin Ballantine dropped down into the chair next to mine and propped his feet up on the rail next to mine. I had on sandals, he wore boat shoes. We both had tall drinks in our hands. Even out here in the open air I could smell his musk oil scent.

"This is nice," he said.

Our vista included palm trees and century plants below, dunes dotted with sea oats, a stretch of pale powdery sand, then the incredible Atlantic. Its color was deepening quickly now, changing from pink to crimson to purple even as I watched. The sky in the east darkened to a deep purple hue as well.

Devin said, "It must have been hard on you girls, finding that body like that."

I put a finger to my lips. "Shush. Melanie has declared the subject of Valentine's murder off limits until after dinner." I was grateful; I didn't want to talk about Val's death with a stranger.

"Good idea. You know, I grew up near the ocean too," he said casually.

"Oh, where?" I asked, turning to give him a closer look. He had black hair and cool blue-gray eyes the color of the ocean on a stormy day; he looked a lot like Mickey. Seeing them together reminded me of the Baldwin brothers, Alex and his younger brother—I couldn't remember his name—William? Alex Baldwin had once owned a beach house on Figure Eight Island when he'd been in a relationship with Kim Bassinger and there were many reported "sightings" of the pair.

"Jersey Shore," Devin replied. "Atlantic City."

Atlantic City, home of casinos and gamblers. Why was I not surprised? Mickey owned a club in Wilmington, near the riverfront. Nick had told me the police suspected him of illegal gambling and drug dealing and were watching the club. Melanie has complete control over her professional life. She used dangerous men to provide the excitement she missed in her life.

Jon had agreed to stay for dinner. Mickey was grilling salmon on an outside grill where fragrant smoke billowed. Jon served drinks from a bar cart, gin and tonics for everyone but me; I was having a soft drink.

Earlier Melanie and Kelly had assembled a lobster salad inside. Melanie offered Spunky nibbles of lobster until, satisfied, he moved to the glass door to stare at his reflection. I wondered if the smell of salmon would lure him onto the deck. "Give him time," Melanie had said when we'd discussed his reluctance to step outside. "He's a house cat. His curiosity will get the better of him and he'll come out. But he'd better not leave this deck; I don't want to lose him."

"They're all working but us," Devin said.

"That's okay. We'll clean up."

I sipped my icy ginger ale. "We grew up on the ICW—the Intracoastal Waterway. You can see our house when you drive over the drawbridge to the mainland."

"You'll have to point it out to me some time."

"Sure. Melanie sold it almost two years ago when our mother got sick."

"Sorry to hear that. Is she okay now?"

"No, she has dementia but with medication she improved enough so that she is able to live with our aunt Ruby in Savannah who is a retired nurse. It was her wish."

"Old age is rough," Devin said.

Another subject I did not wish to pursue with a stranger. "When I was a kid," I said, "I thought the ICW was a natural body of water like the Atlantic and the Cape Fear River. My dad explained how most of the ICW was man made. In the twenties and thirties the Army Corps of Engineers dredged the channel. It starts up North somewhere so that you can sail from the Chesapeake to Florida on the ICW." I reflected that this was something I'd like to do with Nick one day. "Harbour Island, where the Causeway runs from the mainland to the beach, was man made actually. They compacted the sand and clay when they were dredging the ICW and shaped it into an island."

Then I said, "I hear you're shopping for a sail boat."

"Considering one," he replied. "And I hear your husband's away, working for Homeland Security?"

"Yes," I replied. Devin was better at asking questions than answering them. There wasn't anything of a personal nature that I cared to discuss with him. But it turned out that Devin had other things on his mind.

"Mickey was telling me about the trolley that used to bring people out here before the bridge was built. And there used to be an outdoor dance pavilion where the Big Bands played."

"He was talking about Lumina. They even had a huge motion picture screen set up in the surf. But then the war came and it all had to be shut down."

"I'm a bit of a history buff myself and I read that Wilmington was a boomtown during World War Two. They built destroyers here."

"Excuse me," Melanie said, and moved in between us to light a citronella candle that sat on the railing. Darkness was pooling over the Atlantic now and she had lit about a dozen hurricane lamps that were strategically placed around the deck. In the next house, someone was playing show tunes on a piano. Lovely.

"Need any help?" I asked Melanie.

"Everything's under control. You guys go on talking. Dinner's almost ready."

Melanie had on shorts and a matching shirt over a tank top. We all had on shorts. And mosquito repellant on our bare legs.

"Yes, it was a boomtown," I responded to Devin's last question, glad to be on neutral ground. "The shipyard built battleships for the war effort. After the war, the shipyard became one of the state ports. If you're interested in that period, you ought to visit the Battleship *North Carolina*. It's anchored on the Cape Fear."

"Being a historic preservationist you must know a lot about the history of this area. Ever hear about the POW camps that were here during the war?"

"Sure, everyone who lives here knows about them. The first camp wasn't that far from here, Shipyard Boulevard and Carolina Beach Road. But it wasn't large enough to accommodate the prisoners so the government acquired the Old Marine Hospital at Ann and Eighth streets and moved the camp there. And there was a camp at Bluethenthal Field. That's where the airport is now."

"Hold that thought. I'll be right back," Devin said, and got up to refill his drink.

When he returned, I continued, "My good friend Binkie Higgins is an authority on local history. He can tell you anything you want to know. For example, there was an internment camp at Camp Davis. Camp Davis was later absorbed by Camp Lejeune, the marine base."

"A buddy of mine is a civilian contractor at Camp Lejeune. I'll be spending some time with him while I'm here," Devin said.

"What does your friend do?"

"Specialized training. He promised to show me around the base."

"It's good you have a friend in the area," I said. "About the POWs, at first the town was told we were going to get Italian prisoners, but then they sent us Germans."

"How did the people here feel about that?" Devin wanted to know.

"Some were scared. Others relieved. They had heard that the Germans were disciplined and that there wouldn't be any trouble. And there wasn't. If you're really interested in learning more, I'll introduce you to Binkie. He's the expert."

Devin polished off his second drink, or was it his third? "Sure, I'd like to meet him. My granddad used to talk about the war all the time. Seems like it was the biggest thing in that generation's life."

"Tell me something," I asked idly. "Do you own a casino in Atlantic City?" No one ever said what Devin did for a living and I wondered if running a night club was the profession of choice in the Ballantine family.

Devin sputtered. "Me? Own a club in Atlantic City? Donald Trump owns the clubs in Atlantic City. Well, I think he's filed for Chapter Eleven or some such nonsense. But I did work as a black jack dealer in one of the clubs to put myself through school."

"Oh. Where did you go to school?"

Melanie called, "Okay everybody, dinner's ready. We're eating out here, family style."

While we'd been talking she had set the table and placed two big hurricane lamps on it. The table was large and round, large enough to accommodate the six of us and more. White plates were set on colorful placements with rough homespun linen napkins. I started to sit down next to Jon.

"No, over here," Devin called. "Jon, you get to see her every day. I want to feast my eyes on this pretty lady tonight."

He pulled a chair out for me and I had no choice but to sit in it. Then he settled in next to me and turned to give me a frank stare. What gives? I asked myself.

Mickey circled the table, serving us each a salmon fillet from a large platter. It smelled so good my mouth began to water. We passed the lobster salad around and the bread basket.

I sampled the lobster salad. "This is divine, Mel," I told my sister.

She glowed, in her element. Surrounded by her friends, by a man who obviously adored her, she was happy. "Thanks, shug. Kelly made it. Everybody, help yourself to a roll while they're hot?"

Devin leered at me. "I'd like to help myself to a hot roll," he said loudly and we all got the double meaning.

I drew back. Just a few minutes ago we'd been

having a nice conversation. Now he was behaving like a jerk. Was it the drinks?

Jon got up to pour the wine. Jon can't hide his emotions.

He was angry. "How about a roll in the ocean?" he asked Devin. "That ought to cool you off."

"You own this woman?" Devin demanded.

Sensing a fight coming on, I said very loudly, "Stop it! I don't know what's going on here but Melanie has gone to a lot of trouble to give us a nice dinner. I, for one, intend to enjoy it." I looked at Devin pointedly. "If you can't handle your alcohol, then stop drinking." I picked up his empty wine glass and moved it to the center of the table.

"Oh, now she wants to mother me. I can go with that." He laughed suggestively.

Kelly took my cue. "This salmon is to die for, Mickey," she said.

"Oh, don't use that term," Melanie cried.

Jon, still standing, clutched the wine bottle and said, "I agree with Ashley. It's a nice night, good food, none of us died today. So no talk of murder and no hitting on the girls." His eyes shot daggers at Devin.

Devin raised his palms. "Okay, okay. I apologize to everyone and especially to you, Ashley, if I've been out of line."

"Don't sweat it, Dev," Mickey said. "Ashley could do with a little manly attention. Now everybody, let's dig in."

"And what is that supposed to mean?" I asked, outraged, slamming down my wine glass.

"Hey, nothing, Ashley. Cool it. Why are you so hypersensitive? Is this PMS time?"

I started to get up but then realized I was hungry. I wasn't going to miss dinner over a goon like Mickey. "Let me tell you something, Mickey Ballantine, in a few weeks, you'll be history. I know Melanie better than you do. One man is never enough for her."

"Oh, sweetie, that's not true," Melanie said to Mickey and reached out to cover his hand with hers.

Jon was grinning. Kelly looked disappointed that the fight was not over her.

Devin was not giving up. "Ashley, I plan to look at boats while I'm here. Do you think you could find some time to show me around, visit the marinas with me?"

"Well…we start work on Kelly's house tomorrow. But, well, we'll see. I'll try to free up an afternoon." Not on your life, buster, I wanted to say but also wanted the hostilities to cease. I like food and all this fighting was spoiling my enjoyment of dinner.

"Do you think I could tag along to Kelly's house with you?" he asked, and turned to Kelly for permission.

Her fork midway to her mouth, Kelly paused to give him a blank stare.

The phone rang and Melanie excused herself and got up to take it inside.

"Ashley will be working tomorrow morning," Jon said flatly. "She doesn't have time to give you a tour."

Melanie returned and said, "That was J.C. He's coming over for dessert too."

"Good," I said. "I haven't spoken to him since I bought his watercolor and I want to tell him how much I like it." I described the beautiful little watercolor I'd bought just two days ago, glad for the interruption and a chance for people to cool off.

The subject of murder might be off limits during dinner, I thought, but with J.C. and Gordon joining us there'd be no way we could avoid the subject of Val's shooting and the theft of J.C.'s painting from her gallery.

As I ate and enjoyed every bite of my dinner, I couldn't get over Devin's switch from nice guy to obnoxious punk. Mickey was always obnoxious, no surprise there. But Devin had seemed like a decent sort. And something else occurred to me. When people learn that Nick works for Homeland

Security, they ask me a million questions about what he does.

Devin had not asked a single one.

And Devin had not made a play for Kelly as scripted by Melanie and as all men did.

FIVE

WHILE I LOADED the dishwasher, Devin carried in plates and cutlery. He seemed subdued, deep in thought, and made no more passes. When Kelly came inside, he rejoined the others on the deck, their murmuring voices floating inside as he opened then closed the sliding glass door. I brewed decaf while Kelly heaped large servings of her luscious *tiramisu* onto dessert plates and we both dodged Spunky who was constantly underfoot.

Kelly and I chatted easily as we worked, and I complained about Devin's behavior. "He probably had too much to drink," she said, a typical female response to a man's boorish behavior. "Some guys just can't handle their drinks. And Jon does make a potent gin and tonic, long on the gin, short on the tonic."

I wondered why Devin hadn't given Kelly a tumble. Why go for me, the only married person in the group? Because I was a challenge? I wondered.

"I do remember Jon from Biology class," Kelly continued as she mounded cake onto the plates.

"He was cute then and he's even cuter now. Is he seeing anyone?"

"He dates Tiffany Talliere. She's a star on a local soap. But I don't think it's serious."

"That's because he only has eyes for you, Ashley."

I shook my head. "You're mistaken, Kelly, Jon and I are best friends and business partners."

"I know Tiff. We did a shoot together in the spring for *Glamour*. She's a sweetheart. But the way Jon looks at you, she hasn't got a prayer. Trust me, Ashley, I know about these things."

"I think you're just a hopeless romantic," I said, then changed the subject. "About the house, I'd like to get started early tomorrow. I know this is vacation for you but can you meet me there at nine?"

"Sure," Kelly replied, "no problem. I'm used to early calls."

"Want to ride in together?" I asked.

"Can't, Ashley, I've got things to do and you'll be tied up at the house so I'll need my own wheels. Slide the door open for me, will you, while I carry this tray outside."

I slid the door open, saw that J.C. had arrived and was shaking hands with Devin, then I followed Kelly out onto the deck with a tray that bore the coffee carafe along with rattling white mugs and cream and sugar containers.

"Ah, the beauteous Ashley!" J.C. said in greeting and rose to kiss my cheek. "The other half of the gorgeous Wilkes sisters duo."

J.C. could be charming when he chose, and tonight he seemed to choose. "Melanie, summer becomes you. You've been kissed by the sun—oh, lucky sun—and looking more ravishing than ever."

J.C.'s outrageous flattery often made me uncomfortable although Melanie ate up his compliments, seemed to think of them as her due. Still I questioned his sincerity.

J.C. was close to seventy but in very good shape, tall and lean, a runner with the hard ropey muscles of someone who ran marathons. Like the rest of us he had on shorts and a tee shirt, the usual summer beach garb. His hair was gray but abundant, wavy and long, very arty. Most times he wore it bound at the nape of his neck but tonight it was loose and flowing. When it fell in his face, he'd toss his head to fling it back, or else brush it away with a swipe of his hand.

"J.C., what are the police saying?" I asked as I poured coffee and passed out coffee mugs. "Was it a robbery gone sour? Is that why Valentine was shot?"

His response was deliberate, he seemed to be

choosing his words carefully. "They suspect a robbery gone bad, is what my sources tell me. My painting is gone, *finito*. Gone forever. I'll never see that one again, and it was my best. No doubt it's on its way to some unscrupulous private collector even as we speak.

"And poor Valentine, my friend of a lifetime, gone, a senseless crime, a tragedy."

"What else did they tell you?" I asked, dropping down into the chair next to him.

On J.C.'s other side, Devin sipped coffee, spooned cake into his mouth, and regarded J.C. with total awareness. Devin was entirely sober now.

Kelly quietly finished serving the dessert plates then took a chair for herself. It occurred to me that J.C. was barely acknowledging her presence although she had greeted him warmly. But that was J.C. for you, an artist with an artist's penchant for eccentricity. We all strained our ears to catch his next words.

"All the paintings are gone, the entire exhibit," J.C. began. "There were no signs of a forced entry, front and back doors were unlocked, no weapon found on the premises, no witnesses."

"What about the kids who skateboard out back at the gallery? Where were they?" I asked.

J.C. leaned back in his chair, and for a fleeting moment a smug expression passed over his face. It vanished instantly, replaced by a poker face. Having witnessed him holding forth at art exhibits and lectures, I reflected that J.C. loved the spotlight, loved being the center of attention, the last word on every subject. "Kids weren't around this morning. There was a volleyball tournament on the beach so the kids must have been there. No one saw anything."

"Why was the gallery so cold?" Melanie asked. "Did the killer…?"

Mickey pushed back his plate, threw down his napkin, and got up. "Cake was good, Kelly. Thanks. I'm going for a walk, babe," he said to Melanie and squeezed her shoulder as he passed her chair. "Come with me, bro?"

"I think I'll stay," Devin replied, and spooned the last few crumbs from his plate. "That was sensational," he told Kelly.

"The gallery was freezing," Melanie continued.

Jon reached for the carafe to refill his coffee cup.

"I don't know anything about the temperature of the gallery," J.C. said, "but I watch enough true crime shows to know that if you want to confuse the time of death, you keep the body cold."

"So…just as I suspected," Melanie said, "someone turned down the thermostat. I thought it was much too cold in there."

"I'll tell you who the police have in their sights," J.C. confided in a hushed voice. In the flickering light of the hurricane lamps, he reminded me of a shaman in firelight, and all eyes were riveted on him. We were silent, waiting for his next revelation. Out on the beach, the surf built to a high crescendo then crashed on the shore.

"Gordon Cushman's fingerprints were all over the place. I've lived out here for the past forty years, I know every officer on the force, knew most of them when they were kids, they tell me things. And they are seriously looking at Cushman. You see, in preparation for the reception today, Val had a cleaning service in last night. Everything was spotless, so if Cushman's prints were all over the place, it was because he was there this morning."

"You're right! My prints were all over the gallery and with very good reason," Gordon Cushman declared from his position at the top of the steps.

There was a collective intake of air as we all turned to look at him. He had arrived without notice and had heard J.C.'s accusation.

Gordon strode to the table, angry. "I helped Val hang the paintings. I told the police that. I admit I was there. I've got nothing to hide. And I sure as hell did not steal those paintings, then shoot Val. Why would I? She was my friend too."

"Did anyone see you helping her?" Jon asked. "Can someone verify your story."

"It's no story. It's the truth. And no, no one saw me. Val had the shades lowered. She didn't want anyone peeking into the gallery and glimpsing the pictures before she was ready to show them herself. And she had the door locked and the "Closed' sign displayed. The killer arrived after I left and must have worn gloves so he wouldn't leave any prints on the door knobs or anywhere else. The police should be thinking about that, instead of trying to pin this on me."

Gordon was about five-nine, maybe forty or forty-two. His hair was dark but receding and he was developing a paunch around his middle. As long as I had known him he had never been gainfully employed. He'd lived off his wife's book sales while she was alive, and what he was doing for money now I had no idea. Melanie said he was in a jam and needed money. And as everyone knows, money is the most common motive for murder.

Jon, who isn't any more fond of Gordon than I am, got to his feet. "Here, have a seat, Gordon. We've got coffee and cake. Or would you like something stronger?"

Gordon seemed relieved. He moved around the table and took Jon's chair, nodded to everyone, then lifted his face to Jon's. "Got a beer? Sure would like a beer."

"Bring him a beer, Jon, would you?" Melanie requested. "I declare the subject of murder is off limits for the rest of the evening. None of us will be able to sleep tonight with all this talk of murder, and Saturdays are busy days for me. Lots of walk-ins coming into the office and wanting to look at beach properties. So maybe the rest of you can sleep in but I can't. Isn't there something else we can talk about?"

I said to J.C., "I bought your watercolor from Val a couple of days ago. It's a gazebo covered with vines. The style was so simple, yet strong. I love it."

J.C. lifted his coffee mug. "I know the one you mean. That was one of the first watercolors I ever did, back in the days of my callow youth. That gazebo was on the farm our family once owned. I painted it years later, from memory. I'm glad you like it, beauteous Ashley."

Devin said casually, "I'm kind of a World War Two history buff, J.C., and someone said you were a kid here during the war and know something about the POWs that were sent to this area. The whole subject of German soldiers being interned in the U.S. fascinates me. Do you remember them?"

J.C. glared at him. "Maybe the subject fascinates you, Ballantine, but it doesn't fascinate me. You weren't here. You didn't have to encounter those lousy Krauts every day when you were a kid. So yes, I remember them. I remember them too well and I'd just as soon forget!"

We were all silent after that. Poor Melanie, she had been planning this cookout for weeks, ever since she knew that Kelly was coming from New York. As a party it was a bust!

I tried to salvage the situation. "I'm really looking forward to restoring your family's house," I told J.C. "It's a fine example of Georgian Revival architecture from the nineteen-twenties. Those houses were built to last, large and gracious."

J.C. pushed back his chair and got up. "You're wasting your time. Damned house ought to be leveled." He took a few steps, then stopped at Melanie's chair and quickly smiled, instantly Mr. Charm again. "Thanks for the dessert, sweet lips, I've got to run."

"I'll walk you down," she said and left with him.

I stood up too and loaded a tray with the coffee things. "Party's over for me too," I called from the sliding glass door. "I've got an early morning. Night, ya'll." I carried the tray into the house and left it for morning.

Party's over, I thought, and wished it had never

begun. So the police suspected Gordon Cushman, I mused, as I descended the stairs to my room. He said he'd been helping Val hang the paintings, but Jon had told me there'd been a rift between Val and Cushman. And what had happened to Cecily Cushman's estate? She'd been a big true-crime writer, even had movies made from her books, and made plenty of money. As the detectives say, "follow the money," but follow it where? I wanted to know.

SIX

BECAUSE OF ITS UNIQUE architectural significance, the Carolina Heights Historic District was listed in the National Register of Historical Places. The boundaries are Market Street on the south, Rankin Street on the north, with Thirteenth and Nineteenth streets forming the west and east borders. Victorian-era Oakdale Cemetery, the final resting place for four hundred unknown confederate soldiers and countless yellow fever victims, lay to the north of Carolina Heights.

I parked my van on Grace Street in front of the Lauder family residence. The neighborhood was particularly lovely in summer. Shafts of sunlight filtered through over-arching old oaks, spotlighting lilies and peonies and showy front yards. The wide avenue was flanked by sidewalks. Under the watchful eyes of their mother, two little tykes in crash helmets were tearing along on their bikes as fast as their training-wheels would allow them.

It was a cozy residential neighborhood where

young families raised children and seniors took their ease on screened side porches. Every summer there was a block party when the streets were closed to traffic. A nice place to live.

As I waited for Kelly to arrive, I drank in the gracious architectural details of the homes that had been built in the early nineteen hundreds for Wilmington's upper class. Atlantic Coast Line Railroad executives had lived here back in the glory days of the railroad. The pace was slow then and dignified, allowing many of them the luxury of driving home for lunch and a quick nap before returning to their offices.

The architectural styles were Dutch Colonial Revival, Colonial Revival, Classical Revival. And there were Craftsman bungalows too, square and squat with their deep, shady front porches.

Where was Kelly? I wondered, checking my watch. I gazed across the curb to the Lauder residence. It was a gracefully proportioned brick home in the Georgian Revival style. The core of the house was four-square, rising two stories under a blue-gray slate pitched roof with dormers. On the first floor two flat-roofed wings had been added on either side. The left wing housed a glass-enclosed sun porch, the right wing—its mirror image in size and shape—was a screened porch.

Kelly pulled up in a rental car, tooted and waved.

She parked at the curb behind my van. The property had a driveway that ran alongside the house to a detached garage at the back, but as I stepped out of the van I saw why Kelly had avoided it. The concrete was crumbling in many places and tree roots had heaved up whole slabs. On the other side of the driveway lay the remnants of a clay tennis court, overgrown with grasses. If this was any indication of how the house had been maintained, Jon and I had a lot of work to do.

But the front lawn was mowed and the shrubbery pruned so evidently a lawn maintenance service was employed to care for the yard. Kelly verified this as she led the way across the sidewalk. "Mom and Dad keep the old place up, after a fashion. Dad sometimes uses Screen Gem Studios to produce his agency's ads so Mom and Dad stay in the old home place when they're in town. Right now they're traveling in Europe so this is a good time to begin the restoration."

I followed her up the sidewalk to the front door.

"A cleaning service comes in when Mom and Dad are in town to banish dust and cobwebs," Kelly explained as she inserted a large key in the paneled door.

A slight musty odor greeted our nostrils as we stepped inside a formal center hall. The house was hot and stuffy. Ambient daylight filtered through the sidelights and the fanlight over the door, revealing red oak flooring, a worn oriental area rug, and a marred console table.

The finish carpentry was excellent with fine dado below the chair rail. The deep cornice crown molding had been routed into the dentil pattern. But the wallpaper above the chair rail had faded so that the colors were no longer distinguishable and all of the woodwork needed painting.

I was puzzled why, with all their money, Babe and Ted had not taken the trouble to restore the house until Kelly had insisted upon this course of action. My curiosity must have shown on my face because Kelly remarked, "She'd never admit it to strangers but Mother doesn't really like this place."

"She doesn't?" So Babe didn't like the house and J.C. wanted to level it. I couldn't imagine anyone not liking the graceful residence, but then old houses are my passion. I let the matter drop; any further questions would have been impolite. At the same time I caught our reflections in a pitted mirror. Kelly was so golden that an aura seemed to emanate from her very being.

"Help me open the shades," she said, breaking the spell.

On the left, double pocket doors opened into the living room and we moved to the windows there, pulling on the cords of wooden venetian blinds. Blinds like those had made a come back and were very popular today, but these were original, eighty years old. Some of the slats wouldn't turn, the ropes were frayed, but we managed to let in a fair amount of sunlight. And light flowed in from the adjoining sunroom that I'd noted from my van.

"We'll send these blinds out for repairs," I said.

"Oh, why bother? Can't we just replace them?" Kelly asked. She looked around at the overcrowded room with its threadbare rugs and dingy upholstery. "I'd like to get rid of all of this stuff and replace it with reproductions."

I appraised the furniture critically. "You don't want to do that, Kelly. This furniture is authentic, the real thing. These pieces may look bad now but after they've been refinished and reupholstered, you'll be pleased. You've got real treasures here."

"Treasures? What kind of treasures?" Kelly looked doubtful. Was I forever to be regarded as Melanie's little sister? My word and authority disputed because I was once an eight year old tagging along behind sixteen year olds?

"You've got art deco pieces here," I said firmly.

"Art deco? But that's the style of the furniture Melanie has in her house on Sandpiper Cove. And I love the way she decorated her house." Kelly added, "Now that you've pointed it out, I do see some resemblance."

"Melanie and I decorated her house right after she bought it, one summer when I was home from Parsons. But her pieces are reproductions."

"And I love them," Kelly declared. "If you can do something sophisticated like that here, I'd be thrilled." She reached out to give my hand a squeeze. "Melanie was right. You are good."

I smiled, pleased. Kelly was like a different person when they were no men around. "Did Melanie spend much time here when you two were attending high school together?"

"Oh, we were in and out. You know how it is when you're a teen."

"I was just thinking that maybe this is where Melanie developed a taste for art deco and just didn't realize it. You've got a hodge-podge here. Some nicely designed pieces mixed in with what I'd call farm-style furnishings."

Kelly explained, "I think Grandpa Joe moved a lot of stuff in here from the farm after they sold it."

I moved through a large open archway into the dining room and pulled out a chair. I'd been carrying a yellow legal pad and I placed it on the table and withdrew a pen from my shirt pocket. "Let me make some notes, Kelly. Tell me about the house, what you know about its history. The information will help me with the decisions we have to make. We might even apply for a plaque from the Historic Wilmington Foundation."

"Oh, I'd love to have one of those. Sure. I know more about the family history than mother does. Grandpa Joe was always talking about the old days, and I couldn't help but pick up the details. He had a tendency to repeat himself as he got older."

"He was actually your great-grandfather, wasn't he?"

"Yes, my mother's mother's father. That would be my grandmother Peggy whom I never knew. Now she was the queen of high drama if ever there was one, but I'll save that tale of woe for another time."

"Do you know when he bought this house?" I asked, pen poised.

"He had it built, Ashley. In nineteen twenty-five. For some ridiculous sum like ten thousand dollars. Can you imagine? It's worth hundreds of thousands now."

She continued while I made notes. "Grandpa Joe's father was a farmer. He had a big farm not very far from here actually, a hundred acres or so. He had dairy cows and chickens and raised vegetables which he sold. So when Grandpa Joe was young he had the idea to open a grocery store here in town, an outlet for the farm's produce. And it was successful. He and my great-grandmother Marty were already married and their first child, my great-uncle William, had already been born when Grandpa Joe built this house."

"And he lived in it until he died?"

"Lived to the ripe old age of ninety-four. I was twenty when he died, and living in New York with my parents, but during high school, I lived here with him. He may have been old but he was as sharp as a tack. Yet he dwelled in the past; it obsessed him. Especially the war. I think the war must have been a challenging and exciting time for this town."

"And he managed to hold onto this house through the Depression?"

"Yes, and he held onto the grocery store and the farm too. He always told me that our family survived because people couldn't do without milk and eggs so he was able to sit tight until things got better. Then his father died and left him the farm. The whole family moved out there and worked it. They lived at the old farm house during planting season and harvest. Grandpa Joe would get up at four, do the farm work, supervise the hired hands, then drive into town and run the grocery store all day. He was something!"

"He was," I agreed. And probably thought

nothing of it, I mused. People of his generation did what they had to do and did not complain. "So there was your great-uncle William, and your grandmother Peggy, and their mother Marty, and they all lived and worked on the farm?"

"Correct. Now William, there's another tragic story." She shook her head. "Between William and Peggy and their problems, then losing his wife Marty when she was in her prime, Grandpa Joe must have hit rock bottom. But he held onto his sanity by devoting himself with a passion to the family he had left and the farm and the store."

"How does your uncle J.C. fit in?" I asked.

"J.C. is not really my uncle, he's my great-uncle. He's William's and Peggy's younger brother. About twelve years younger than William. Let's see, Uncle J.C. is only ten years older than mother so that would make him sixty-nine."

I scribbled on my pad. "He was born in nineteen thirty-six?"

"Sounds right. The war started in nineteen forty-two and Marty died in nineteen forty-seven. She had become reclusive, staying out at the farm almost full time. All the farm workers had gone off to war so she had a big job on her hands. Grandpa said she worried terribly about William and working the farm seemed to distract her."

"How sad," I said.

"Yes it was. You see, William was reported MIA, that's 'missing in action,' then later was reported as taken prisoner. My family has had a lot of grief. You can see it in my mother's face. She's always got that sad glint in her eyes.

"What saved the farms were the German POWs the government brought to Wilmington. They were a godsend to the farmers. They worked on the farms, helping the farmers. So my great-grandparents had the hands they needed to save the farm. And even though William was a prisoner of the Germans, and strange as it seems, Marty got very attached to those German boys."

Kelly gave her long silky hair a shake. "Doesn't make sense, but that's what Grandpa Joe told me. He said she might not have lasted as long as she did if it weren't for those young men. She made sure they had good dinners and took an interest in them personally. You know, many spoke English and were educated. Marty told Grandpa Joe that she was looking after them in the hope that a motherly German woman was looking after William."

"She sounds like a good woman," I commented.

"She was. But I think Uncle J.C. resented the attention she gave to the prisoners; that's why he sounded so bitter last night."

I looked around the room and asked, "Do you happen to know when this furniture was acquired?"

"I do. Grandpa Joe told me, quite proudly, that he bought everything new when they moved into this house. He said he didn't want to bring old furniture into a new house. But when the farm was sold—some developers bought it in the fifties to build houses out there and it brought a lot of money—Grandpa moved things from the farmhouse in here, pieces that had sentimental value. He just couldn't part with them. That's why everything's so crowded and such a jumble. By then my great-grandmother Marty was gone and Grandpa didn't care much how things looked."

SEVEN

KELLY AND I MOVED from room to room and I made a list of the furniture we would refinish and those pieces we'd donate to Habitat for Humanity.

"Art deco had a tremendous influence on the furniture designers of the twenties, whether intentional or unintentional," I told Kelly. "Suites of furniture became popular." I indicated the living room sofa and club chairs. "See how they all match. And they were designed to be multi-functional. Those arms open out to form end tables." I demonstrated.

"But the upholstery is so scratchy," Kelly complained. "I used to avoid this room because of the scratchy upholstery."

"It's mohair," I said. "We'll replace it. Today's mohair is as soft and lustrous as velvet."

"Grandpa's favorite spot in the house was the library." She led the way across the center hall and into the library that was opposite the living room, and pointed to a leather club chair with a humidor positioned on a table to its right. "That was 'his' chair. Even after all these years you can still smell the cigar smoke. I used to sit in here with him after school and we'd catch up. He'd puff on those smelly cigars and relate the family history and recount what life had been like in the war years."

One wall of the room featured built in bookcases and a fireplace. The fireplace had been converted to gas with gas logs. On the end wall, a door led out onto the screened porch.

Then something caught my eye. "Oh, my. Look at this wonderful floor lamp." Positioned behind the leather club chair was a wrought iron floor lamp. The base of the lamp was a snake standing on its tail. Its head and neck were coiled and supported the glass globe.

"Ooooh, I always hated that thing," Kelly said.

"It's a gem," I said. "If you don't want to keep it, we can sell it to a collector in a heartbeat."

"I'll think about it. I'm starting to see these things through your eyes, Ashley, and I have to admit they are looking better."

"Do you have any ideas for the color palette?" I asked.

"Well, I like what you did in Melanie's house. Something soft like that."

"We used taupes and ivories, peaches and aquas in her house. In a place this size I think we ought to add some deeper tones, maybe some burgundies, so that the rooms don't appear to float. What do you think?"

"Peaches and burgundies? Sounds pretty. Ready to see the upstairs?"

Light from a clerestory window illuminated the staircase. On the landing I spotted a long jagged crack in the plaster that looked like it might be serious, and made a note of it on my pad. "We'll refinish the stairs and install new carpeting," I said. "I think a runner with brass rods on each tread would look good and serve well. Maybe a small pattern, in peach and brown."

Kelly's fingertips had been trailing the rail and she turned to smile at me. "Ashley, I think I'm just going to leave those decisions to you. You know what you're doing, you don't need me second-guessing you."

"Bless you," I whispered under my breath. The perfect client.

There were four spacious bedrooms upstairs and one very large white tile bathroom. Each bedroom had a fireplace, making a total of seven fireplaces in the house.

"I want you to see Marty's room. Grandpa kept it like a museum. They once shared it but after she died, he moved into the bedroom across the hall."

The bedroom was actually quite modest, suggesting it had been lived in by a woman with simple tastes. There were plain white curtains on the windows. The radiator between the windows was uncovered. The walls were painted pale blue. Furniture that must have come from the farm was simple and useful, an iron bedstead, a pine dresser and chiffonnier.

Kelly gave the mahogany-stained closet door a yank. "It always sticks," she said.

"Old houses like these have settled," I said. "We'll give the foundation and floor joists a good thorough check."

Kelly pulled a flat box down from the closet shelf. "These are papers of my great-grandmother's I'll have to go through."

She set the box on the white chenille bedspread and lifted the lid.

"Oh, look at those old-fashioned dress patterns," I said.

Kelly removed a portfolio and opened it to a sheaf of pencil drawings. "These must be Uncle J.C.'s early drawings," she said. "I'll have to go through them and ask him if he wants them." She put the lid on the box and returned it to the closet.

"Look, Ashley, I know it's an imposition, but there are things I'm going to want to save, items like that." She indicated the box on the shelf then closed the closet door. "Do you think I could store a few boxes at your house till I have a chance to look at the contents? I don't feel comfortable imposing on Melanie to store them for me in a rental house."

"Sure, Kelly, that'll be no problem. I'll take that box with me today, if you want. I'll be stopping by my house later to check on it."

"That'd be great. I'll be back over here tomorrow afternoon to go through Grandpa Joe's desk. Melanie said she'd help me box up items like sheets and blankets and take them to Goodwill. The clothing is so out of style and worn, I don't think even they would want it."

I dragged open the closet door again, took down the box, and set it on the bed. Glimpsing the crowded closet, I did not envy Kelly having to go through her great-grandparents' personal belongings. I remembered how difficult it had been when Melanie and I had had to dispose of our mother's personal possessions. And remembering the difficulty of such a project, Melanie had volunteered to help her best friend get through it.

We moved into another larger bedroom that must have been the one Kelly's parents used when in town. She showed me the room that used to be hers when she was in high school, sweet and girlish with flower-sprigged wallpaper and Priscilla curtains.

"We've got to find a place for a second bathroom up here," she said.

"And install central air-conditioning," I said, fanning my face with my legal pad.

"I've about had the heat here too." She glanced at her watch. "I've got to get going." We descended the stairs to the cooler first floor and I walked her to the door. Impulsively, I hugged her. "Thanks for selecting me, Kelly. I'm going to enjoy restoring your house."

She hugged me back. "I'm really excited about what we're doing, Ashley. It's going to be beautiful. I'm looking forward to spending more time in Wilmington once the house is done."

As we said goodbye, she said, "Oh, I almost forgot. Here's a set of keys," and handed a key ring to me. "We had very secure locks installed on the doors and windows after Grandpa Joe died. Mom, Dad, and I were living in New York so the house was often empty. Are you staying?"

"Yes. My camera is in the van. I'll take pictures and measure the rooms. I have lots of notes to make. See you later at the beach house."

I watched her drive away, retrieved my briefcase with the camera and measuring instruments from my van, and went back inside the house which was getting hotter by the minute. As I passed through the rooms I turned on the fans and reflected that moving hot air felt cooler than stagnant hot air.

Alone in the house, I had to admit it felt kind of creepy. Houses have personalities of their own and to me this house felt conflicted. Open, loving, homey, yes, yet at the same time secretive. I'd had my own house blessed after I'd restored it and I thought it a good idea to recommend that Kelly do the same. Let the house start a fresh chapter in its life just as the residents might do. To that end, I measured and photographed, and made many notes in the legal pad, singing an old tune under my breath, *Where Have All the Flowers Gone*, my favorite anti-war song. From my dad I'd inherited an eclectic collection of fifties, sixties, and seventies music.

As the heat grew more intense I hurried through my examination of the second floor, scouting the rooms for a place to install a second bathroom. If we gutted two closets that backed up to each other, we might just carve out space for a small bathroom.

My tee shirt was sticking to my back, and I lifted it to get some air. It was then that I heard sounds coming from the first floor. Someone was down there, walking around. I'd left the front door standing open to allow some fresh air to enter the house.

I went to the top of the stairs and called down. "H-e-l-l-o? Kelly? Somebody down there?"

Only eerie silence met my ears. I grabbed up the box containing the dress patterns and drawings from the bed and hurried down the stairs with it. I made a tour of the first floor but there was no one there. I locked the front door carefully behind me. Had someone in the neighborhood walked in? Maybe a nosy neighbor? But why then hadn't he or she responded when I called down? Or waited to speak to me?

EIGHT

"I'LL HAVE THE Crab Melt Sandwich," I told the waiter at the Oceanic Restaurant.

Our gang had overslept and we were having Sunday brunch at the oceanfront restaurant. I'd called Jon and he'd met us so there were six of us then Gordon Cushman showed up and he made seven. It turned out Melanie had invited him. "I'm so glad you could come, Gordon sweetie," she cooed. Melanie was up to something. She doesn't get mushy over people unless money is involved.

The day was hot and hazy. Our table was positioned at the window on the top floor and overlooked the beach, the ocean, and the pier. Outside everything was blue: blue water faded into blue sky and the horizon was a blur. Strollers on the beach moved slowly, and even the waves seemed sluggish, not pounding the sand forcefully, just laboriously rolling ashore.

Mickey was in a sullen mood but that seemed to be habitual so nothing new there. Kelly was quiet as was Devin. Gordon Cushman seemed more nervous than usual. I caught him watching Mickey when Mickey wasn't looking.

Melanie was hyper, as if as hostess to this merry little band she had to make up for everyone else's lack of vitality. Thank goodness I had Jon; without him I might have set fire to my hair and run out of the building screaming.

Hot coffee and iced tea restored us. Kelly complimented Melanie on her outfit, a colorful cotton shorts and halter set in a tropical pattern. "It's a Tommy Bahama," Melanie said, "that I picked up at Redix. I've got to take you there, shug. They've got everything. And great sales."

Jon's omelet arrived and smelled and looked so good I almost lifted it off his plate. But then the waiter set my crab melt in front of me, and I forgot all about eggs. Pale yellow cheese oozed between slices of grilled rye bread. I picked it up and took a greedy bite.

"I like a woman with an appetite," Devin said.

There he goes again, I thought.

"You know what they say, a woman who likes food likes sex too."

"Give it a rest, will you?" Jon said testily. Poor Jon. He was usually so easy going but Devin was really getting on his nerves. And mine.

Gordon glanced at Mickey warily then said to Melanie in a rush, "I want you to sell my house for me." Gordon was a fashion plate himself in his khaki shorts that rode low under his belly and his white athletic socks with stripes at the tops.

"Which house? Your beach house or the town house?" she asked and didn't seem a bit surprised.

She knew this was coming, I realized. My sister's antenna had been quivering for days in response to Gordon's financial problems. So she'd been expecting this to happen.

Gordon cleared his throat and mopped his forehead. "No, no, not the beach house. I've got to live here. The house on Orange Street." He had not even touched his Shrimp Lover's Platter, but kept darting surreptitious glances at Mickey. Idly, I wondered if he'd notice if I reached over and snitched one of his plump, fried shrimp. Better not. Melanie might smack my hand.

"I can sell that house in a heartbeat," Melanie said confidently. "It's beautifully restored and I have a buyer who is looking for a house just like yours."

Melanie used that line all the time with clients while she courted them. After the listing agreement was signed, the buyer mysteriously did not materialize.

"Why don't we drive downtown this afternoon and I'll take a look at it? Then I'll go back to the office and do a comp survey." She bestowed Gordon with a dazzling smile. "You were right to come to me. I'll get you top dollar."

Melanie is very successful and this little exchange proved why.

"That pier gets worse every time I see it," Jon muttered, staring out the window at the wooden pier below.

The first third of the pier was used by the restaurant for outdoor seating and seemed solid enough. But beyond the dining area with its white vinyl chairs and white vinyl tables, a barricade had been erected to close off the remaining two-thirds of the pier. A large warning sign was posted on the barricade.

"It undulates like a snake," Jon complained.

Devin turned in his chair for a better look. "Guess the storms got to it. Glad they've got up that barrier."

After we each paid our checks, I told Melanie, "Jon and I are going out on the pier. I'll see you back at the house later."

"Sure, shug. Gordon, let's take my car. I'll drive. You relax."

I smiled to myself as I waved them off. Relax? Poor Gordon, he didn't know what he was in for.

As we climbed the ramp alongside the restaurant, I said to Jon, "I think this vacation may rob me of my sanity."

"Then move out," he said irritably. "I don't trust that Devin. He's trouble. Move back home. It's closer to the work site anyway and you wcn't have the drive into town every day."

I stepped out onto the pier. "Oh, I know you're right, Jon, but Melanie's been planning this group-living adventure for months. She really wants me there, and, well, you know, she is my sister. I can't let her down."

He shrugged. "Well, watch yourself with Devin."

We had reached the barricade by then. "Danger," the sign read in big bold red letters. "Pier closed. No trespassing."

Peering through a large opening in the barricade, I saw how the pier humped up then rolled down. A section of the railing bowed out over the water. "One of the waiters told me he'd climbed out there on a dare and it swayed under his feet."

"The next hurricane will finish it," Jon predicted.

NINE

"I'M SO WORRIED about Nick. I haven't heard from him all week," I confided in Jon as I crumbled cornbread with my fingers then devoured the crumbs. I tend to eat when I'm upset. When I'm happy. When I'm bored. I just like food.

Usually Jon makes excuses for Nick but tonight he said, "He shouldn't be doing this to you, Ashley. I can't imagine going off and not calling my wife for a week, especially if that wife were you. But he's done this before. Remember when he was transferred to Atlanta? He was supposed to call, then he just left you hanging, high and dry."

"But that was over a year and a half ago, Jon, before we were married. He hasn't done anything like that since. Besides, he explained about what he was going through in Atlanta, that terrible case he had to solve."

"He neglects you, Ashley. When he isn't travel-ing, he's taking intensive language courses at the

University. Can you honestly say that you two ever spend time together?"

"Sure we spend time together," I said defensively. "In May we celebrated our first anniversary and shared a wonderful evening. And then in June we went out for my birthday."

"June? That's the last time you shared an evening? I have news for you, Ashley, your birthday was over two months ago. This is not how happy marriages are made!"

Duh! I was speechless. Was this my buddy Jon speaking?

Our waiter approached to take our orders and I was glad for the distraction. Everything Jon had said was true, and nothing I hadn't told myself. Yet hearing it from someone else seemed—disloyal.

Jon had taken me out for Sunday night dinner at Savannah's Restaurant on the Causeway because he thought I had to get away from the crowd at the house, especially Devin. He told me I needed cheering up but so far he wasn't doing a good job of it.

"What about the other times he traveled on assignment for Homeland Security? Did he call then?"

The waiter brought the wine Jon had ordered. He uncorked the bottle ceremoniously, then poured a small amount in Jon's glass. Jon tasted, approved, and we were served.

"Nick called faithfully. Every night. And after that month-long assignment he had with the Department of Energy at the Livermore Lab in California last October, his trips have been short. Workshops and conferences mostly in the D.C. area. He'd be gone for a few days, then back. Mostly weekends."

Jon was frowning. He'd become very protective of me of late. I felt the same way about him. I always felt like I had to protect him from the women he got involved with, like they might take advantage of him. He was so good-hearted and guileless, wore his heart on his sleeve, and was as transparent as a bride's negligee: an easy target for an unscrupulous woman.

Our entrees arrived, Benne oysters for Jon, jumbo sea scallops for me.

"It's true that after he returned from California, they had him studying Arabic so he could help translate documents and recordings. He took classes all winter and spring at the University, very intensive, and he played tapes in the car and carried a tape player around with him. But that just gave me more time to work with you on our restoration projects." I smiled. "It's a wonder he didn't speak Arabic in his sleep.

"Nick discovered he had a gift for languages, something he didn't know about himself. Then this summer he started making short trips to CIA headquarters to translate some cell phone messages, what they call 'chatter,' that they had intercepted. But he was never gone for more than three days and he called regularly. So you can understand why I'm worried now. I'm about ready to get in my car and drive up there and haul him home!"

Jon grinned. "I can just see you storming the ramparts at the CIA! Let me know when you're going. I'll go with you."

I laughed.

"Well, what happens when you call him?"

I shook my head. "I just get his voice mail. I leave messages but he doesn't return my calls. I can't help thinking that something is wrong."

"Have you tried calling CIA headquarters?"

I set my fork down. "Storming the ramparts would be easier! You can't imagine how hard it is to get to an operator. They've got the most complicated recorded menu. I almost gave up in frustration. Finally I got through to a real live human being. I asked to be connected to Nick Yost but she just asked me for an extension. When I didn't know his extension, she told me that without the correct extension she couldn't connect me."

"That is frustrating! And Nick didn't leave you an extension number?"

Shaking my head pitifully, I murmured a pathetic, "No."

JON INSISTED ON picking up the dinner check although I offered to share. As we stepped out onto the breezy causeway, he said, "Ashley, I think you need to have some fun. Do something to take your mind off worrying about Nick for a few hours. And I know just how to cheer you up."

"How?"

"Come with me." He opened the passenger door of his new Cadillac Escalade and I got in. "We'll return for your van later."

We drove east on the causeway to a beach club. I heard the music as soon as I climbed down out of the SUV. I was glad I'd changed outfits earlier. I had on black walking shorts, silver sandals, and a silk camp shirt in fuchsia. Large silver hoops dangled from my ears. I slipped my hand into his.

He held on to it. "They're playing our song."

"My favorite," I said. *I Love Beach Music* by the Embers flowed into the parking lot, making my body want to move.

Inside, the floor was packed with dancers of all ages from teens to seniors. On the Carolina coast, the shag is universal. Summer day camps teach it to children.

Jon got us two beers from the bar and set them on a table. He grabbed my hand and pulled me onto the dance floor. His palm on the small of my back was warm and firm. His shoulder felt solid under my left hand. I slipped my right hand into his left. We moved in close in the traditional slow-dance position just as the DJ segued into Percy Slege's *When A Man Loves A Woman*. Slow and easy. Wildly romantic. It'd been a while since I'd shagged but the steps came back easily.

When the DJ moved on to *My Girl* by the Temptations, Jon murmured in my ear, "We're good together, Ashley."

I pulled back and looked him fully in the face. Uh oh, I didn't like where this was going. "Best partner I ever had," I said and gave him an innocent smile.

He didn't say another word, just drew me closer.

When Melanie and I were growing up, Daddy and Mama used to shag with us at home on Saturday night when Melanie didn't have a date, which did happen once in a while. We rolled back the rug in the living room and turned on the stereo to one of the beach music stations out of Myrtle Beach or Elizabethtown. Daddy taught me the steps, counting out loud, "One, two, one, two, rock back, rock forward." Mama danced with Melanie. She was as tall as Mama; you almost couldn't tell them apart. The same flowing auburn hair, pale oval faces, yellow-green eyes. Remembering, I smiled to myself.

Jon returned my smile, thinking it was meant for him. "I've worked up a thirst." He lead the way to our table. I was lifting the glass to my lips when his cell phone chirped. He pulled it out of his shirt pocket and checked the incoming number. "They're early," he said, as if I'd know what he was talking about. I didn't have a clue. Who's early?

As Jon said, "Hi, Wayne," my own phone rang. We exchanged raised-eyebrow glances. I lifted my phone from my waist band. The number seemed vaguely familiar.

"Ashley, we need you. They're coming out tonight," said a woman with a rich Southern drawl.

"Hi." I didn't know who I was talking to.

"It's me. Betty."

"Oh, Betty! Hi. Give me a minute. The music's loud in here."

Jon held his phone to one ear, his palm cupped the other. We moved to the exit, away from the noise of the music and the crowd.

Betty Matthews, I thought. All of a sudden I

knew why she was calling and what Jon had meant when he'd told me, "They're early." Turtles don't generally hatch until September, and this was still August.

Betty said, "Tonight's the night. We need your help. On the beach in front of Gordon Cushman's house. That doggone fool's got every doggone light in his house turned up megawatt high. Wayne's on his way up there now to read him the riot act, and trying to reach Jon Campbell at the same time. Can we count on you?"

"Jon's here with me. We'll be right there. We're not far."

"We're on our way," Jon told Wayne.

Then we exchanged grins, joined hands, and sprinted to his vehicle. "Turtle watch!" we sang as we jumped in.

He sped over the bridge that crossed Banks Channel, turned left onto Lumina Avenue, then topped the speed limit all the way to Gordon's house. It was well after midnight and there wasn't any traffic. If one of the Wrightsville cops stopped us, he'd be sure to give us a police escort when we explained our mission. On our own, we made it in two minutes flat.

"Here, take these." Jon unloaded flashlights and two broad industrial brooms from the back of the Escalade.

We scooted around the side of the house and waded through the sand to the boardwalk. The beach-side lights had been extinguished. From the top of the boardwalk, I spotted Betty and Wayne Matthews down on the beach. I practically skipped down the steps, realizing I'd been humming a tune Daddy used to sing, *Pack Up Your Troubles in Your Old Kit Bag and Smile, Smile, Smile*. It felt good to be doing something useful.

"I thought Cushman would never come to the door," Wayne complained as we crossed the sand toward him. "He's wasn't asleep. Had every doggone light on in there and outside as well. Place was lit up like a landing pad."

"We're gonna have to help them," Betty said as we joined her and Wayne on the strand.

I looked up into the night sky and saw why. Cloud cover. The moon slipped in and out of dense clouds. And no stars. Jon quickly flicked his flashlight over a spot in the sand marked with yellow flags. "There's the depression. They're moving around down there, starting to dig out. The sand's shifting downward." He switched the beam off.

"Okay, let's all get into position," Betty directed. "Wayne, you take the big flashlight and go down to the water's edge. Shine it across the strand, aim the light up here at me. Ashley and Jon, start sweeping. Go, people!" Even as she spoke, Betty was smoothing the sand in front of the nest, clearing the runway.

Jon and I took our brooms and ran toward the water, smoothing the sand as we went. Something as small as a human footprint could trap a baby turtle.

"Val should be here with us," I said.

"I miss her too, Ashley," he replied, sharing my pain.

"Here they come!" Betty called.

More than a hundred baby loggerheads, each no larger than a man's thumb, scrambled out of the nest in what is called "the frenzy" and began their life and death race toward the brightest horizon. This should always be the tide, lit up by moon and stars, but with man's encroachment, on overcast nights turtles often confused the bright lights of cottages and street lamps for the ocean.

Jon and I were positioned on either side of the runway. We'd swept an obstacle-free path for their escape. Our presence would keep raccoons and other predators away. Wayne held his beam steady, and the first of the marathon runners scrambled swiftly past our feet, heading straight for Wayne's light and the ocean beyond. A hundred or more hatchlings followed in one surge, crawling over each other in their haste.

Sand near my foot dimpled. A crab. He peeped out of his hole. An early breakfast, he supposed. I moved a warning foot toward him. Down he scuttled. "No feast this time, Mr. Crab."

The mother of this brood, a loggerhead about my own age, had hatched in this exact same spot twenty to thirty years ago. Before she left the nest, she imprinted its exact location on her brain. No one knows how loggerhead females do this. This big mama was the one in ten thousand loggerheads who had survived to become an adult. If her luck held, she could live to be a hundred. I did some quick calculations and realized that in order for the environment to produce one adult loggerhead, the scene we were witnessing had to be replayed one hundred times. No wonder loggerheads were an endangered species.

In two minutes, their flight was complete. The hatchlings who didn't drown—turtles are air-breathing creatures—and who hadn't been eaten by predators would continue to swim for twenty-four hours until they reached deep, safer water.

Wayne, Jon, and I danced up the beach to Betty. We linked arms and frolicked around the empty nest, like Druids dancing around a bonfire. We hugged and kissed. "We did it! We did it!" we cried, jumping up and down.

"They did it," Wayne said soberly.

"I'm beat," Betty said. "It's way past my bedtime. Wayne and I will come back in the morning and excavate the nest, just in case a hatchling got left behind. If we find any, we'll free them when it gets dark. You two go on home." Betty hugged and kissed me. "Thanks, Ashley. I like having you out here at Wrightsville. This is where you belong, child."

Jon kissed Betty and shook hands with Wayne. Toting broom and flashlight, the Matthewses started their trek south along the ocean's edge to home and bed. Jon picked up our brooms and we moved toward the dunes. "You sleepy? Want to stay a while."

"My adrenaline's pumping. I'm wide open."

"Wait here, I'll get a blanket. We can sit out here and talk and maybe the stars will come out."

I watched him disappear around the beach house. In a minute he was back, spreading a blanket in front of a dune. I slipped off my damp sandals and sat, legs folded under me. Jon dropped down close and leaned back on an elbow. For a while we listened to the surf wash in and out, the soothing rhythm slowing our excited heartbeats. I pictured a hundred and fifty baby turtles, their tiny legs pumping against the tide, their little heads surfacing for air. God's creatures. Go, little turtles, I silently prayed. Grow into big mamas.

"It's so peaceful here," I said, stretching out on the blanket.

"It doesn't get any better than this. Ashley, I agree with Betty. It is nice having you out here at the beach. So close by…" He didn't reach out his arms, but he pulled me to him just the same, a pull as strong as the moon's pull on the tide. He face loomed above me. I knew he was going to kiss me.

"Jon, no, wait." I took a deep breath. "We can't. Let's just…wait. I don't want things…our friendship… Besides…"

"Besides. There's Nick. You're married. You're right, Ashley. I'm sorry."

"Forget it. We got caught up in the moment. Look at the stars," I said.

He stretched out on the blanket next to me. We held hands. Overhead the clouds had parted, revealing a celestial canopy of stars. Their brilliance hushed even the roar of the ocean and stilled my throbbing heart.

Just as I started to relax, a bright flicker of light to the right caught my eye. "What's that?" I cried.

"Fire!" Jon yelled. "A bonfire. And a big one. They can't do that. There's an ordinance against open burning. Come on." He sprang up and gave me his hand. We ran down to the water where the sand was packed, then sprinted toward the fire.

The large bonfire was out of control. "Somebody's there. I can see a man," I said.

A man was racing around the bonfire, carrying something. I wasn't sure what he was doing until we came right up on him.

"Gordon! What in the world are you doing?" I shouted.

"What does it look like I'm doing?" he shouted back angrily. "I'm putting this damned fire out."

He did have a shovel and he was scooping up sand and throwing it at the base of the flames. "We should call the fire department," I said. But there seemed to be no time.

Furiously, Jon and I began scooping up sand in our hands and piling it at the perimeter of the fire. The heat was intense. A stack of short sticks was burning, and something else that curled like sheets of paper—canvas? Were they soaked in turpentine or something? They popped and exploded.

I spotted a child's sand pail and rushed to the water to fill it, then ran back across the beach to pour water on the fire. After many trips, and when the fire seemed to have run out of fuel, it slowed, then died.

Jon and Gordon heaped piles of sand on the embers.

"Why the hell did you start a fire, man!" Jon exploded.

Gordon wiped sweat from his brow with his sleeve. Flinging the shovel down on the sand then dropping down beside it, he said, "Are you crazy, Campbell? I didn't start it. I was trying to put it out."

"Well, what happened? Who set the fire?"

"I was getting ready for bed when the blaze caught my attention. I threw on some clothes, grabbed a shovel and ran down here. Would have called the fire department but my battery is dead. There was someone here and I hollered to him, but he ran off before I could see who he was."

"Sorry for the misunderstanding," Jon said. "No hard feelings?"

Gordon reached up and they shook hands. "No hard feelings. And thanks, Ashley." He got up wearily and brushed sand off the back of his shorts then stumbled off toward his house.

Jon and I trudged slowly back up the beach, collected the blanket, and he drove me back across the bridge to get my van, the only vehicle left in the parking lot outside Savannah's Restaurant.

I said, "I wonder what that person was burning. I'm going out on the beach early tomorrow and dig up whatever it was. Some type of accelerant was used. I saw the way those pictures…pictures! That's what they were."

"Are you sure? I couldn't tell."

"I think so. Want to meet me?"

"You bet. I'll be there. Seven?"

"Seven."

We hugged goodnight. Even sweaty, Jon smelled good.

TEN

Someone had brewed coffee. Its fragrance drew me up the stairs and into the kitchen. I filled a white mug and carried it out onto the top deck where I found Devin Ballantine in a chair pulled up to the railing, feet propped up on a lower rail. I lifted a hand to shade my eyes from the sun and looked him over. He had on shorts and a blue tee shirt. His hair was damp from the shower, curly, almost black. His lashes were long and luxurious. I knew women who would kill for lashes like that.

I was glad I'd slipped on a long tee shirt over my bikini. I didn't want Devin drooling over me again. "Good morning," I said crisply.

He gave me a big smile. "Hey there, sleepy head."

"Sleepy head? It's only seven."

He got up and dragged another chair over to the rail. "Here you go. Sit next to me. Don't you look yummy in the morning."

Oh, don't start, I wanted to shout. And for pity

sakes, wash off that overwhelming musk cologne, I wanted to add. For a second he had sounded almost human. He took a sip of his coffee, then said thoughtfully, "You were out late last night. Melanie was worried about you."

"Oh, I rather doubt that," I said sharply. "Melanie and I stopped keeping track of each others' hours years ago."

"Well, she was wondering where you were. She said it wasn't like you to stay out late when you were working."

That sure got my hackles up. This guy had a way of getting under my skin. "Are you asking me to account to you for my time?" I asked indignantly.

"Whoa!" Devin said. "Let's start over. Good morning, Ashley. I hope you slept well." He smiled disarmingly.

I laughed. "Oh, what the heck. It's no secret. I was on turtle patrol." I told him about my adventures with the loggerhead hatchlings.

"That sounds like fun. And useful. I'd like to go with you next time. Would you call me?"

"Sure," I replied, "We always need help." I set my coffee mug down on the table and put on sunglasses. "Going for a walk," I said as I moved to the flight of stairs that led down to the beach.

Devin sprang up. "Want company?"

I hesitated, "Well, I am meeting Jon."

"Oh, Jon won't mind if I tag along."

He sure was thick-skinned.

I hesitated a moment, then decided to tell him about our mission. I explained about the bonfire and that we had decided to see what someone had been burning. "It wasn't driftwood," I said. "Driftwood doesn't burn like that."

I could see I'd piqued his interest. "I saw a rake in a storage room under the house. Let me get it."

With Devin carrying the rake, we trudged up the beach, passing early morning runners and strollers, many of whom I recognized and greeted with a "hey." No dog walkers though; pooches are banned from April to October and I miss the little cuties. Most dogs are better behaved than most children, I mused, and we don't ban them. As we passed J.C. Lauder's house I saw him out on the deck, doing yoga. I waved.

"I think that position is called the tree," I mentioned to Devin. J.C. was standing on one foot, the other foot lifted and pressed into his thigh. His hands were joined together high over his head.

"He's sure got good balance for an old guy," Devin said, looking back at J.C. "Still hasn't moved. I'd be hopping around on that one foot."

Devin wasn't bad when he stopped putting on a front.

"Bet you could do that," he said then. "You've got great legs."

I stopped abruptly and turned to him. "You never give up, do you, Devin? You know, I think that basically you're a nice guy but you've got this Casanova complex and think you have to hit on women to prove your manhood or something. As of right now, you are going to stop hitting on me. Otherwise, I'm going to have you kicked out of my sister's house!"

Devin's mouth dropped open. "Wow, you are something. Okay, okay, you win. I apologize." He switched the rake to his left hand, shook hands with me with his right. "A truce?"

"You're on," I said.

Over his shoulder I saw J.C. watching us. We continued our walk. "So you think someone was burning pictures," he said casually. Too casually. I gave him a look. What was he up to? Devin Ballantine was an enigma. A regular guy one minute, charming even, a jerk the next.

"Maybe the stolen pictures?" he pressed.

"I don't know, Devin. But yes, that idea did occur to me. They burned like they'd been soaked in an accelerant. But wouldn't the oil and turpentine on the canvas act as an accelerant?"

Devin looked thoughtful. "Seems that way to me."

Jon was waiting for us. Like Devin he'd had the

foresight to bring a rake. "What's he doing here?" he asked me, not even bothering to conceal his hostility.

Devin stood the rake in the sand. "Ashley has pointed out that I've been acting like a jerk, Jon. Sorry."

Jon looked at me. "He wants to help," I said.

Jon wasn't convinced. "Hmm" was all he said, then pointed to the bonfire site. "Tide washed out a lot of what was here. I managed to unearth a few items."

He indicated a pile of debris at his feet, then lifted a charred object and handed it to me.

"I'll take this down to the water to see if I can wash off the ashes," I said.

When I returned, they were hunkered down, poking around in the pile. I showed them what I'd found. "It looks like the corner of a frame. See the gilt."

Devin looked up into my face, serious now. "Some of these fragments do look like canvas. I believe someone was burning paintings. These must be the stolen paintings from Valentine's robbery."

Jon frowned. "But that doesn't make sense. Why would someone steal them, then burn them?"

"Did you bring your cell phone, Jon?" I asked. "We've got to report this."

Jon withdrew his cell phone from his pocket and

called Officer Meriweather who was heading the investigation for Wrightsville PD. Folding his phone closed, he said, "He'll be here in a few minutes. Asked us to stay with the paintings…stuff, whatever it is."

We walked down to the water's edge, searching for additional fragments of frames and canvases in the tide. Devin remained at the bonfire site. I searched the sand but didn't find anything new.

The sun rose higher, pure and golden.

"Is he really going to tone down the rhetoric?" Jon asked, referring to Devin.

"I think so. It was all an act, like he's got something to prove. Don't ask me. What I know about men could fill a thimble."

"Still no word from Nick?" he asked gently.

I shook my head. "No. Something's wrong, Jon, very wrong. I don't know where to turn."

"What about checking with the chief of Wilmington PD?"

"I've already tried him. He said he hasn't heard a word, that Nick doesn't report to him any longer. He's worried too."

Jon turned. "There's Hank." Officer Meriweather was striding across the beach.

We both looked to the bonfire site. "Where the hell did Ballantine go?"

Devin was gone.

ELEVEN

I LEFT JON TO DEAL with Officer Meriweather whom he knew on a first name basis. As a permanent resident of the island, Jon knew all the members of the PD. I had to hurry back to the cottage to get ready for work. The sun was heating things up as I trudged down the beach to the south end. I passed a family of sun worshippers, children happily building a sand castle with dad, mom shiny with oil; she and her miniature, a pre-teen daughter, were stretched out in beach chairs.

Where had Devin disappeared to? I expected to see him sitting out on the deck when I climbed the outside stairs, but he wasn't there, and I didn't see him as I passed through the great room. The man was sure a puzzle. I didn't see anyone, not Melanie nor Kelly as I helped myself to more decaf. I wondered if Kelly had already left for downtown. She was meeting Jon and me at the house at nine. I had to hustle.

I showered and dressed in what Melanie refers to as my "construction wear chic," khaki shorts with a multitude of pockets, a tee shirt, and steel-toed construction boots with thick socks. A roofing nail through a sandal is no laughing matter, despite how Melanie scoffs at my attire.

Jon's Escalade and Kelly's rental car were already parked at the curb in front of the house on Grace Street when I arrived. A heap of black plastic garbage bags lined the curb.

Kelly and I had made a thorough tour of both floors of the house on Saturday. This Monday morning had been reserved for inspecting the basement. The house was hot and stuffy and I was hoping the basement would be cooler.

"Because of the cracks I've seen throughout the house," I said as I snapped on the lights at the top of the basement stairs, "I'm expecting to find some damage down there."

"Oh no!" Kelly exclaimed as she led the way. "Don't say that."

"Don't worry," Jon said soothingly. "There's a solution for every problem. We'll handle it. We work with an excellent, experienced general contractor and we'll bring in specialists."

I surveyed the large gloomy space. The foundation was made of cinder blocks and I moved closer to one wall to inspect its condition. "Just as I suspected. Cracks," I said as I shone my flashlight on one.

"Fixable," Jon said, joining me. "We'll repair the cracks and apply a sealant."

"We'd better have a radon test just to be on the safe side," I said.

"Radon? What's that?" Kelly asked in an alarmed voice.

"Radon is a naturally occurring gas that is found underground. If it's here it may have seeped into the house through these cracks. It could be dangerous."

Oh, for the life of a New Yorker, I mused, high above the ground in an apartment, and let someone else worry about things like basements.

"Don't look so glum, Kelly. This stuff is minor," Jon said.

"The cement floor is in good condition," I commented. "Basically, it's dry down here. Looks like someone started remodeling. That paneling is real knotty pine, tongue-and-groove, used for paneling walls in the days before sheet paneling was manufactured."

A carpentry project had been started, then abandoned. One wall of the cinder block foundation had been covered with golden pine tongue-and-groove boards. A portion of the ceiling had been covered as well.

"Great-uncle William did that, way back when. He had the idea of making a rec room down here, a place where he could escape from the rest of the family. Grandpa said that when Uncle William returned from the war, he had been restless and nervous. Working with his hands helped him stay focused."

"But he never finished it," I said, examining the carpentry work which was exacting. "He was doing a nice job."

"Well, you know," Kelly started, then hesitated, then finally blurted, "Uncle William committed suicide."

"No, I didn't know. I'm sorry," I said.

"Well, it was all very sad. He was a basket case after the war. Grandpa referred to his condition as shell shock; many veterans returned with post-traumatic stress syndrome. After he took his life Grandma Marty started going downhill fast. She died too, a year later. Poor Grandpa."

"You said your family history was tragic, Kelly. It surely is," I said sympathetically.

I thought it would help her to get the conversation back onto a professional note. "Well, I don't see any signs of asbestos insulation. In a lot of old houses it was used to insulate furnaces and boilers. It's that stuff that kind of looks like white cloth covering plaster. And if it's friable—that is crumbling—you're in trouble. But none of that here."

"And your water pipes are made of copper not

lead," Jon said. "That's very good news. You're lucky. Let's plan to update the plumbing and electrical."

"Sure, go ahead. Do what has to be done."

"I think we've seen enough," I said. "Let's go back upstairs."

In the center hall, Jon said, "Kelly, you don't need to hang around. You must have more important things to do. We've got people coming to start removing the furniture."

"The refinishers, like we discussed," I said to Kelly. "And a truck from Habitat for Humanity is coming to take the items you said you don't want to keep."

"I went through the personal stuff over the weekend like you asked, Ashley. That's what all those bags are out there at the curb. And I packed up some things and they are being shipped to New York to mother and dad's apartment. But here," and she moved into the library, "here are some things I'd like you to keep at your house for me. I just glanced at this stuff, but I want to go through it slowly when I have time. Do you mind storing them for me at your house? It's just temporary."

"Not at all, Kelly. There's really not much here. I'll put them away for you till you're ready. Looks like photo albums."

Kelly picked up an album. "Old pictures." She flipped through the black pages. Black and white photographs were mounted with tiny corner tabs onto black paper. Captions were written in white ink. "Here's a picture of the POWs who worked the farm that I was telling you about Ashley."

I peered at a photograph of about a dozen young men, all with closely cropped hair, dressed alike in work shirts and dark trousers, and wearing some sort of identity tags. Under the photo, someone had written their names with white ink. The handwriting was perfect schoolgirl penmanship.

"I think my grandmother Peggy made these albums. I don't want to part with them. I want to go through them with mother. She may be able to tell me who some of these people are."

She lifted a second box. "And this is full of Grandpa Joe's personal correspondence and I want to read through everything."

I took the box from her and carried it out to my van. Jon carried the box of photo albums and shoved it in the back. "I'll put them in a safe place," I told Kelly. "You can come look through them any time you want."

We said goodbye and she drove off. "Is it my imagination or does that girl seem a mite frail to you?" Jon asked.

I considered the question. "For a New Yorker,

and for a super model, yes I do. Wonder if this tendency toward melancholia is inherited."

WHEN I OPENED THE DOOR to my house a wall of heat hit me. I set the boxes on the floor, then tapped in my code on the alarm system pad and the red light stopped flashing. The next thing I did was lower the thermostat. Oh for blessed air conditioning. However had the people of Wilmington survived their summers before air conditioning?

It was a little past four and check-in time at The Verandas Bed & Breakfast down the street had begun. The three-story structure was listed on the National Register of Historic Places as the "Benjamin W. Beery House." During the Civil War, Captain Beery had constructed a monitor on top of the roof where, with the aid of a telescope, he spied the Cape Fear River for Yankee ironclads.

As I sipped iced tea and watched from behind the lace panel at my parlor window, a steady stream of cars pulled up in front of the beautifully restored Italianate mansion.

I turned around and savored the wonderful feeling of being at home. I'd been gone for less than a week and being back made me realize how much I missed my cozy house. And how much I missed my husband who had moved into my house after we were married.

I'd bought it two years ago from a reclusive woman who'd been transferred to the nursing home where my mother had been a patient. I have a master's degree in historic preservation from the Savannah School of Art and Design. My undergraduate degree, a Bachelor of Fine Arts, had been earned at Parsons School of Design in New York.

After college, I'd formed a partnership with Jon to restore old houses. He'd worked with me to restore my own house back to its Victorian condition and the effort had been a true labor of love and very satisfying.

My colorful house, with its equally colorful history, was one of the oldest on Nun Street, built in 1860, two years before the Civil War. A plaque next to the front door, issued by the Historic Wilmington Foundation, identified it as the "Reverend Israel Barton House." Reverend Barton, a Quaker minister, had been the first owner, and he'd had a secret room constructed where he'd hidden runaway slaves. The pastor and Mrs. Barton had raised nine children in this house and it defied logic for me to figure out where they had put them all with only three bedrooms and one bathroom upstairs.

I'd had my house blessed by Father Andrew and when the work on the Lauder house was finished I intended to suggest to Kelly that she do the same. Although her house exuded warmth and friendliness, I sensed that some sort of underlying conflict had occurred within its walls. I wondered if William Lauder had committed suicide inside the family home and if that episode had caused the chill in the atmosphere I had sensed.

Carrying my iced tea I walked down the hall to my favorite room, the library. Cozy and warm, the heart of the house. We'd painted the walls here with three coats of red paint and an artist friend of mine had stenciled Dutch metal leaf *fleur de lis* designs to suggest tooled leather. Heavy velvet draperies, tied back on either side of lace curtains, blotted out some of the intense sunlight and heat. Shoulder-high built-in cherrywood bookcases flanked the fireplace, and there was a compartment for firewood.

On the floor I had overlaid richly colored Oriental rugs. I trailed over their thickness now to regard the watercolor I'd hung on the wall only a few days ago. My garden had its own gazebo that was original to the property; it was covered with Carolina jessamine that bloomed profusely in the spring with bright yellow trumpet-shaped flowers. The vines shaded the gazebo year round.

I picked up the phone and invited Binkie out to

the beach house for cocktails. He accepted readily and I sensed he was lonely. "I'll pick you up in about thirty minutes," I told him. "I have to water my plants and go through the mail here. Then I'll come get you."

"Can't wait to see you, dear girl," he replied.

TWELVE

BINKIE ADMIRED our ocean view and declared he was quite impressed with Melanie's "cottage." Melanie, Kelly, and Mickey were not at home but Devin was expecting us. He poured white wine for Binkie and then for me when I said I'd have a little. Then we three leaned back and stared at the ocean, transfixed by the gently rolling surf. Talk could wait as we unwound.

When the pianist in the next house began to play, Binkie smiled, his fair skin crinkling, his seventy-year-old blue eyes as bright and keen as a seventeen-year-old's. "Ah, Gershwin," he declared. "A medley from *Crazy For You*."

"I recognize it," I said. In the spring, on one of the weekends when Nick had been away attending a Homeland Security workshop, Jon and I had driven to Raleigh to see *Crazy For You*, one of the Broadway South Series at BTI.

"*Embraceable You*," Binkie said and smiled, identifying the romantic song being played. He had on soft chino pants and his faithfully-worn brown suede Hush Puppies. A blue short-sleeved shirt accented the blue of his eyes. His silver hair gleamed. Binkie's hobby was boxing and it had kept him fit for seventy plus years.

As a Professor Emeritus at UNC-W's History Department, he knew more about the history and folklore of the Cape Fear region than anyone. He had authored many a scholarly book on the subject. With his friends—with everyone—he was kindly and gracious, a Southern gentleman of the old school.

As if reading my mind—and sometimes he does—he reached out and patted my hand. His hands were worn like everything else about him, but offered reassurance and comfort. After Daddy died, Binkie stepped into my life and I leaned on him. He seemed to need someone to need him, for he had never married and had no family. Recently Melanie and I had learned that our Aunt Ruby had been the love of his life.

I was proud of him and said to Devin, "Binkie can tell you anything you want to know about wartime Wilmington."

To Binkie, I explained, "Devin is something of a history buff."

Devin seemed comfortable with Binkie and me and I remarked to myself that the stern talking-to

I'd given him that morning seemed to have had a positive effect. He was courteous and friendly, and thank goodness, not flirtatious.

"I'm particularly interested in whatever you can tell me about the German POWs who were interned in this area," Devin said.

Binkie likes nothing better than to discuss our town's history with someone who is genuinely interested. "Let me start at the beginning. The first German POWs to arrive in North Carolina were sailors who were rescued from a sunken U-boat off our coast in May 1942. The survivors were taken to Fort Bragg."

Devin listened intently and did not interrupt, something I knew Binkie appreciated. I refilled their glasses from the wine bottle; one was enough for me.

"The War Department—that's what the Defense Department used to be called, but you probably know that."

Devin nodded.

"The War Department set up seventeen internment sites across the state for the captured German, Italian, and Japanese prisoners. Many of the early German prisoners were members of the elite Afrika Korps."

"I understand there was a camp downtown in the heart of the city," Devin said.

"You're referring to the converted World War

One Marine Hospital at Ann and Eighth Streets. The prisoners there were Germans who worked in the fertilizers plants and on the farms. Under the terms of the Geneva convention, the POWs were provided living quarters and rations on a par with our own armed forces. So life for them wasn't bad. They had work for which they were paid, but were permitted to keep only eighty cents a day. They were well fed and received medical services when needed. In their free time they could play musical instruments, read, paint or draw, plant gardens, or engage in their beloved soccer games."

"What were the relations between the town and the prisoners?" Devin asked.

"In a word, cordial. Some of the prisoners became quite attached to their farmer employers. Years after the war, they maintained a correspondence. Some of the Germans even returned here to visit."

"Did any escape?" Devin asked.

"Few prisoners ever attempted to escape so although there were guards security was not heavy. The farmers themselves were permitted to drive a truck into town and sign out their workers for the day."

Binkie grinned. "Now there is the story of one prisoner who escaped from Camp Butner, made his way to Chicago, and lived there for fourteen years without being detected. That was extraordinary. Generally, the very few who did escape were found and returned."

"But not all?"

"No, not all."

I got up and picked up the empty wine bottle. "I'm making sandwiches. Binkie, will you stay and eat with us?"

"I'd enjoy that, Ashley," he replied graciously.

I left them to their discussion and went inside. Spunky wrapped himself around my ankles and complained loudly. "Miss her, do you? Well, how about some tunie?" His ears twitched at the word.

I popped the top on a can of tuna cat food and scooped it into his dish. Then I was forgotten by my feline friend. "You've sure got us trained well, Spunky," I said to the top of his head.

When I returned to the deck with a platter of turkey sandwiches, chips, and soft drinks, Binkie was saying, "Interestingly enough, the prisoners remained in Wilmington for almost a full year after hostilities ended with Germany. During that year, they continued to work the farms, often without guards. In early nineteen forty-six they began to leave and by April they had all been shipped out. We heard that many didn't want to leave, that they asked to stay, to become U.S. citizens. But there were war reparations to be made and they were sent to England to work the farms there for another year or two."

"Did they all make it safely home to Germany?" Devin asked.

"Who can say?" Binkie said mildly. "Who can say."

"Okay, guys, enough war talk. Let's eat. And then I'll drive you back to town, Professor Higgins."

"I enjoyed our little chat," Binkie told Devin as he poured himself a Diet Coke. "Thank you for all you've told me," Devin replied. After dinner I drove Binkie to his little bungalow on Front Street, kissed him soundly on the cheek, told him I loved him, and headed back to Wrightsville. The house was dark and empty. Devin had gone out. I went around turning on lights, filled Spunky's water dish, and went back out on the top deck with a tall glass of iced tea.

The moon was sailing high, the stars were coming out, and I felt very, very small and alone. I looked up into the night sky and thought, those stars are shining down on you, Nick, wherever you are. My emotions were conflicted: hurt that he hadn't returned my calls; fearful that he hadn't called because he was injured—or worse; angry with him for doing this to me.

We'd been married out there on the south end of the beach, a year and three months ago on the first Saturday in May. The wedding and the reception, and an ocean-view cottage for a two-week honeymoon had been Melanie's gifts to us. The beach cottage had four bedrooms, four bathrooms, and a high-tech kitchen where Melanie's caterer friend Elaine McDuff and her crew prepared the wedding feast. There had been a spacious greatroom with a wood-burning fireplace for cool nights. My cheeks burned as I recalled how Nick and I had made love with complete abandon in front of that fire.

I'd worn my mother's wedding dress. I'd lost enough weight so that it fit and it was beautiful with a train that trailed behind me over the white runner that had been rolled across the strand.

As I'd kissed and thanked Melanie for making all the wedding plans, she'd confessed that she'd probably never marry. She had grinned wickedly. "I like playing the field. The grass is always greener, and all that. Marriage would cramp my style."

Marriage had not cramped my style, I reflected. I liked the cozy feeling of belonging to someone. I wanted a family, to fill my house with children, oh not the nine children the Bartons had raised in my house, but two or three. At first I thought I'd conceive right away, but it's hard to get pregnant when your husband travels and is a workaholic when at home. Romantic evenings didn't come often enough for me in our house.

Reliving my wedding day, I remembered how I had floated down the stairs to Binkie who was giving me away. He'd gasped when he saw me, tears shining in his eyes. "Oh! Ashley dear, you're beautiful."

"It's Mama's dress," I said shyly. I wasn't comfortable being the center of attention. "I'm nervous," I confided.

Behind me, Melanie said, "She'll be fine."

Binkie said, "I happen to know that Nick is a nervous wreck, and Jon, his best man, isn't much better." He offered me his arm. "Shall we go out now, Ashley dear, and settle their nerves?"

"Yes," I replied.

Melanie had led our procession across the boardwalk and over the dunes, looking elegant in a pale blue gown. Watching her step daintily onto the white runner, my heart overflowed with love for my older sister who, when the chips were down, was always there for me.

Guests turned in their folding chairs to watch Melanie march slowly and rhythmically toward the ocean as a recording of Pachelbel's *Canon* played.

A white canopy had been erected midway down the beach, and the tails of gigantic white bows fluttered in the ocean breeze as playfully as the tails of a child's kite. Huge white baskets held mounds of white hydrangeas, and they were banked at the edges of the white carpet that covered the sand under the canopy.

The sun was setting, casting red and gold rays over the scene and tinting white foam to pink. In the east, the horizon had deepened from bright blue to indigo.

When the music switched from Pachelbel to *Lohengrin*, people rose up out of their chairs, oohing and aahing. Binkie said in my ear, "Ready?"

I whispered yes and we started down the aisle that was formed by Nick's friends and mine, toward Mama and Aunt Ruby who were in the first row.

Then I caught sight of Nick, waiting expectantly under the canopy, and I felt that everything was going to be all right.

But was it all right I asked myself? If my marriage was what I had expected, I wouldn't be sitting out here on this deck by myself asking these questions. I'd be sound asleep, secure in the arms of my husband.

Sighing loudly, I got up from my chair, tidied up the kitchen, and went downstairs to my room. I was the only guest to have a suite of my own. And of course like every other room in the house it was decorated in white—white walls and carpeting, a white wicker desk in the sitting room with a white leather sofa. But a black wrought iron canopy bed dominated the bedroom with a white tailored comforter and shams.

I heard a car door slam under the house and someone came up the stairs and let themselves in. A moment later there was a tap at my door.

"I'm glad you're still up," Kelly said when I opened the door. "I brought you a present."

"A present? For me?" I was delighted. How sweet of Kelly. She set a Palm Garden shopping bag, with its signature palm tree, on the sofa.

"Go ahead, open it," she laughed.

"You shouldn't have," I said. Why do people always say that as they are ripping the package open?

Kelly pulled out the desk chair and sat down at the desk. She unfolded a blue and green map as I thrust tissue paper out of the bag.

"I picked up a map of Wrightsville Beach," she said. "I don't have a good sense of direction so it helps me to look at places on a map. Good thing I live in New York where you only have to be able to count street numbers to find your way around."

I withdrew a dress from the bag and held it out. "Kelly, this is beautiful!" I exclaimed.

She turned away from the map. It was one of those freebies given out by Intracoastal Realty and you saw them everywhere. "I thought it would look good on you. You can wear it tomorrow."

"My first Lilly Pulitzer," I said as I admired a colorful sundress. Pink and green designs on a white background. Silk and chiffon. Spaghetti straps, a flirty flared skirt.

"It's so summery," I said. "I love it."

Kelly picked up the map, then laid it back down under the lamp. "Why is the north end of the island called Shell Island? I always wondered about that."

"It used to be a separate island," I replied, and moved to a mirror to hold the dress up in front of me. "How did you know my size?"

"You're an eight, right?"

"I am. Hurricane Hazel filled in the inlet separating Shell Island and Wrightsville with sand. They became one island."

Kelly got up, leaving the map spread out on the desk. "I'm glad you like the dress. Wear it tomorrow."

I kissed her goodnight. "Thanks," I said, "you're sweet."

How had I ever thought Kelly was a pain? I wondered to myself as I drifted off to sleep. She was a lot like Melanie, unpredictable but basically kind and generous.

THIRTEEN

THE NEXT MORNING, Tuesday, I went to work early, met with the plumbing contractor, then left before noon to drive back to the beach house to shower quickly and change into the sundress.

"Ready?" Kelly called, passing my door.

When she saw me, she exclaimed, "I knew that dress was meant for you. Look at her Melanie, doesn't she look sensational?"

"Sensational!" Melanie agreed. "Too bad that wandering husband of hers isn't around to see her."

"Well, thanks a lot, Mel, I really needed to hear that."

She put her arm around my waist and drew me toward the exit. "Sorry, shug, but I'm getting a mite annoyed with the elusive Detective Yost." To Kelly she said, "I never really wanted Ashley to marry him but she was so in love. And he does love her, I know that. He's just always so preoccupied with work stuff, I have to question his priorities."

I glared at her. "Will you two will ever stop talking about me as if I'm ten!"

"Sorry, Ashley," Kelly apologized. "She's right," she said to Melanie. I groaned. Even when they were trying not to they still talked about me as if I were not present.

"Well, let's get going. I'll drive," Kelly said, and we left in her rental car.

The Louise Wells Cameron Art Museum at Seventeenth Street and Independence Boulevard was our destination. The museum is dedicated to preserving and exhibiting North Carolina Art but houses an international collection as well. We browsed through a permanent collection of Mary Cassat color prints that depicted the daily rituals in the lives of nineteenth century women: bathing fat chubby babies, writing letters, serving tea.

The museum was cool and I was glad I'd brought a cotton sweater to drape over my bare arms. But the dress was pretty and I felt pretty in it.

Next we looked at Claude Howell paintings. Howell was a Wilmington native, and fascinated with the effects of our coastal light which he thought was unique. He painted scenes from local life, a beach cottage and a fisherman in bold blues and greens, a picture of two fisherman sorting fish in dusty pinks and blues.

There was a landscape of the falls in Cherokee County by William Frerichs that reminded me of the Hudson River School exhibits I'd seen at the Metropolitan Museum of Art.

"Uncle J.C.'s press conference is at one-thirty," Kelly said. "Let's grab a quick lunch while we can."

"A glass of chardonnay," Melanie told our waitress in The Forks Restaurant inside the museum.

"Same for me," I said, and Kelly asked for one too.

After the wine came and Melanie said, "To us," I ordered the Southern Style chicken salad. Melanie and Kelly decided to try the Cornbread Salad, made with cornbread croutons.

"At the end of the day, they're crating Uncle J.C.'s paintings and he's shipping them to Christie's. They've been on temporary loan here since the museum opened in 2002. I think he knew that something like this Christie's auction would come along."

"He'll be set for life," Melanie declared. "And he deserves it. He's worked hard all his life producing these paintings. He only brings out one or two a year, so you can see how much time he puts into each one."

"Not only that," Kelly said, dipping her fork into her salad, "well, Melanie knows this but I don't think you do, Ashley." She paused.

"Know what?" I asked.

She said importantly in a hushed voice. "Uncle J.C. and my grandmother Peggy were the ones who found William's body."

"No!" I exclaimed, my mouth open, my fork midway to it.

"Yes. They found him hanging in the barn at the farm. That's what sent Peggy over the edge into oblivion and sent my great-grandmother Marty into declining health. She died within a year after William's death. And the shock of the discovery made Uncle J.C. the way he is. You know, difficult, mercurial. One moment he's flattering you to death, the next he's speaking to you contemptuously as if you were an idiot."

"Can you imagine?" Melanie said. "The Lauders have sure had their share of troubles."

"Well, mother and I have made good. Now it's J.C.'s turn. And I agree with Melanie, he deserves it."

"Who deserves what?" a voice asked.

I looked up guiltily to see J.C.

Kelly giggled. Melanie, who is never at a loss for words in any social situation, said, "You deserve the adoration you are receiving, J.C. Come, sit with us."

"How can I refuse a chance to be seen with three beautiful ladies. Kelly, sweetheart, how are you darlin'?" He pecked her on the cheek then sat down in the fourth chair.

"Now what have you girls been up to?" His brown eyes surveyed us suspiciously.

"We were just discussing the work on the house," Kelly said, flustered. "It's going to be beautiful. Ashley's having the nineteen-twenties furniture refinished and reupholstered."

J.C. turned his piercing gaze on me. "Now is that a fact? We'll just have to throw a big party when the house is restored, now won't we?"

"Maybe we can get the house on the Olde Wilmington by Candlelight tour this year," Kelly said excitedly. "What do you think, Ashley? Can you put a word in the right ears?"

"I'll certainly try. And we'll be finished by then."

Kelly leaned across the table. "Uncle J.C., we found some of your early drawings in a portfolio in your mother's room."

J.C. was thoughtful for a moment. "Is that so. Why I'd like to see them, darlin'. I'm getting so forgetful I can't even remember any drawings that are not in my possession. Where'd you say you found them?"

"They were in great-grandma's pattern box," Kelly said brightly. "Ashley's storing some boxes for me because she has the room and I don't."

"Well, at your convenience, then, Ashley. I'd better run, girls. They're waiting for me. See ya'll later."

We finished lunch then strolled through the museum to the gallery where J.C.'s paintings were on display. He was in the middle of an interview with two television journalists and their cameramen. J.C. stood before one of his paintings as he answered their questions. "I began painting seriously when I was fourteen, although I'd dabbled in drawing and watercolors as a child."

J.C. Lauder was often compared to Andrew Wyeth. They were both American Contemporary Realists. They had painted at about the same period, the late forties and fifties especially, and then continued to work throughout their lifetimes, although Wyeth had been born twenty years earlier than J.C.

Their subject matter was similar—weathered barns, farmhouses, people who made a living off the land—but Wyeth's paintings portrayed the cold northern climate of Pennsylvania with snow covered ridges and leafless trees, while J.C.'s paintings depicted the warm southern light that Howell was so enamored with.

Our own North Carolina Museum of Art owned an Andrew Wyeth painting that I always paused to examine when I visited the museum in Raleigh.

Called *Winter 1946* you could almost count the blades of frozen grass on the hillside in the picture.

I wandered around the gallery as the press conference continued. There was a painting of a dairy barn and I felt jolted. Had this been the barn where J.C.'s older brother William had committed suicide, where J.C. himself and his older sister Peggy had found him?

There were several portraits of a young woman, fresh and smiling, with lovely brown hair and warm brown eyes. "My grandmother Peggy," Kelly said at my side.

"She looks so happy," I said, surprised.

"I think those were done before the troubles," Kelly replied.

I considered how that might have been, mulling it over.

FOURTEEN

WEDNESDAY MORNING WAS HOT and muggy and I hated leaving the beach where there was a breeze off the ocean. In town, steam seemed to rise from the pavement. I pulled up in front of the Lauder house at about eight to find that Willie Hudson, our elderly general contractor, had already assigned a crew of brick masons to the project. How pleased the neighbors must have been to awake to a construction crew on their street.

The brick masons had erected scaffolding across the front of the house. All the windows in the house had been pried open, and someone looked down at me from one of the upstairs bedroom windows. Good old Jon had beat me to the site again, I thought, although I didn't see his Escalade parked at the curb. I waved but by then he had moved away.

The brick bonds on the Lauder house had been laid in the English pattern design which had been popular in the twenties. Brick was beautiful and durable and provided excellent insulation.

"Hey, Miz Wilkes," Willie called and came to meet me on the sidewalk. "Or should I be callin' you Mrs. Yost? And what do you hear from that hero husband of yours?"

"Hey, Willie," I called back. "When are you going to start calling me Ashley?"

"When you start calling me Mr. Hudson." He grinned a big toothy grin. This was our morning ritual.

"Okay, then Mr. Hudson, I've decided against the hyphenated last name. Ashley Wilkes-Yost sounds too much like Ashley Milque-toast to suit me. So I'm sticking with Wilkes."

Willie threw back his head and roared with laughter. "Milque-toast! That's a good one, Miz Wilkes. Anybody know you would have a hard time thinking of you as Milque-toast. Not the way you keep findin' bodies."

"Let's not get started on that. You've begun the pointing, I see."

"Sure have. Took off all them old gutters and leaders yesterday, and will have new ones up before the end of the week. This nice hot weather's just fine for pointin'."

"You like this weather?" I asked, incredulous.

"Love it. I was born in the summer, partial to summer ever since."

"Are you finding much damage to the mortar?" I asked.

"In a house this age, and with settling and all, the mortar's cracked pretty good. Some pieces are just plain missing. So my boys take a chisel and a hammer and chip away the loose mortar. They'll slosh water into the joints so them old dry bricks don't suck up the moisture out of the mortar. Then we'll trowel the mortar into the joints and be as good as done.

"And while we're up there, we'll be looking around for missing or cracked bricks. Got a stack of new ones up there just so's we can replace the old. Selected them myself, match just fine."

"Sometimes I wonder why folks bother to hire me and Jon, Willie. You know more about this than I'll ever know."

"That's what I keep askin' myself, Miz Wilkes," Willie laughed. "But then, you gotta do all that paperwork. Myself, I hate the paperwork."

"Okay, well, I'll see you later. I'd better get inside and see what Jon is up to." I started to the door, moving backward up the sidewalk.

"Mr. Campbell ain't in there," Willie said, giving me a puzzled look.

I turned toward the front door, then turned back

as his words stopped me. Something flashed directly in front of my face and hit the step with a loud thud.

Willie was at my side in a flash and I didn't know he could move so fast. He was hollering like mad, yelling for his crew.

"What was that?" I asked, feeling slightly dazed. I looked down. A brick.

"You crazy fools!" Willie was bellowing and looking up. "Watch what you're doing up there. You almost hit Miz Wilkes!"

His fists were clenched; laid-back Willie was furious.

A face appeared overhead, peering down from the scaffolding. "What's wrong, boss?"

A second face appeared near the first.

"Don't you boys ever toss bricks off that scaffold, you hear me! Don't you got no sense?"

"We didn't toss no bricks, boss. No sir. Not us."

Willie looked stumped. He pulled off his hat and raked the front of the house with his eyes. "Well, somebody done tossed that brick."

"Somebody here? No," I said. "Maybe one of the loose bricks fell off the facade." I nudged the brick with the toe of my boot. It didn't look cracked or worn. In fact it looked new.

"Well, who's in the house?" I asked. "Who's here?"

"Ain't nobody here but us," Willie said and frowned.

"But I saw someone up at the window," I insisted. "I thought it was Jon."

"I told you. Mr. Campbell's not here. Nobody here but us. Let's check the house."

Willie and I and the two brick masons who had scrambled down off the scaffolding to join us made a thorough search of the house. We found no one. But the back and side doors were open and the screen doors were not latched. Anyone could have come in and left by the back door, unseen. But why? I asked myself.

Willie studied me like he was seeing me for the first time. "You done got yourself involved in another murder, Miz Wilkes, and somebody tryin' to kill you!"

FIFTEEN

COULD WILLIE BE RIGHT? I asked myself as I tried to sleep that night. Had someone deliberately thrown a brick at my head? At night things always seem gloomier and more dramatic than they do in the clear light of morning. At one a.m. I gave up trying to sleep. I got up and took my cell phone off the charger and dialed Nick's cell phone number. But all I got for my effort was his voice mail and I suspected he had his phone turned off so he could sleep.

As I should be doing, I told myself. But the thought of going back to bed to those twisted sheets and tossing and turning in them was just too appalling. I unlatched the sliding glass door and slid it open. The air felt and smelled wet and salty. I loved hearing the soft whoosh of the breakers. If I could sleep out here, the ocean's song would put me to sleep faster than any lullaby. But it would simply be unsafe and foolish to sleep out on an open deck.

If only Nick were here with me, then the bed

would be heaven, not hell. I stretched out in a lounge chair on the deck and thought serious thoughts, the kind that plague you only at night. Jon was right. This was not the way marriage should be. This was not how I had envisioned my marriage. I had married a police officer with my eyes wide open, yes, and I had been willing to be patient with Nick when he was working a difficult homicide or putting in double shifts. But this Homeland Security liaison position was far more demanding, a situation I had not bargained for. And if Nick was no longer working for Wilmington PD, then who was he working for? When he did return home, I planned to have a serious talk with him about us, our marriage, and our future.

I remembered how Jon had almost kissed me on Sunday night. And how I'd almost let him. Jon and I were compatible; we had so much in common. There were times when we seemed to read each other's minds. If I were married to him, I would not be suffering this way. We'd have an idyllic life together, working on exciting restoration projects every day, making a home together—Jon was as interested in the domestic arts as I was—Nick couldn't care less what a room looked like. One thing was sure, I wouldn't be sleeping alone.

Out on the beach an insomniac like myself was

strolling in my direction. He, or she, disappeared from view behind a dune. I got up and went back inside, securing the glass door behind me. Unable to face that disheveled bed again I stretched out on the sofa. I plumped up the cushions, arranged them under my head and shoulders, and pulled the chenille throw over me.

I had just drifted into the first stages of sleep when something woke me. Light. A shaft of light from behind me. Had someone opened my sitting room door from the hall?

I lay still and listened. Someone was walking stealthily behind the sofa where I was hidden from view. Should I jump up and confront whoever it was? Turn on the light? Chase him out?

But what if he was dangerous? Not a member of our household but an intruder? A burglar? Might he not attack me?

I ruled out Melanie; she would not be sneaking around the house. She would have snapped on the lights and called my name. I pressed myself down into the cushions and listened.

Someone crossed the room and went into the bedroom. I saw a faint flashlight beam moving around the bedroom and heard objects being moved, drawers being pulled open. A robber?

As I was wondering if I should slip off the sofa and

crawl to the hall door and escape, the door to the hall opened and a second person came in. Two burglars?

The second person tiptoed past the sofa where I drew myself into a tight ball. The back of the sofa concealed me, and the white of the chenille throw blended in with the white upholstery. The second intruder crept into the bedroom.

Someone gasped and yelped. Then I heard a thud and sounds of a scuffle. What in the world was going on? I dared not move. I scarcely breathed. But my ears were straining to hear every sound.

Then one of them ran past the sofa, threw open the door, and raced down the hall. His footsteps were muffled by the thick carpeting, but I felt sure I heard him leave the house by the outside stairs.

Another person went flying through the sitting room and out into the hallway. Slowly I got up and tiptoed to the doorway. A lamp on a console table gave off a little light. They were gone. I closed the door firmly and pushed the button lock.

Silently I moved to the glass door to the deck. I unlatched it and dragged it open a foot and stepped out. Ducking down, I sidled over to the railing.

Two figures were running on the beach. From the distance they could have been male or female, I couldn't tell. They were running north, toward the Oceanic Pier that loomed out over the ocean.

Should I call the police? I asked myself. But then I'd be up for the rest of the night and I hadn't had any sleep at all. Tomorrow was a work day. I needed to be up in—I looked at the clock—five hours.

I turned on the lights and searched every inch of my suite to make sure I was alone. The bed was a jumble with tangled sheets and humped up pillows and those people—whoever they had been—might have thought I was in the bed, sleeping soundly. Had they intended to harm me?

I recalled what Willie had said, that someone was trying to kill me. I examined the bed closely. It was just as I had left it. The mattress was not pumped full of bullets. The pillows were not slashed to shreds by someone wielding a knife. No one had attacked the bed where they thought I slept. So this was not about me.

And the first person had shone a flashlight around the room, searching for something. What did I have that someone would want to steal?

I checked the lock on the hall door. Secure. For good measure, I dragged a chair up against it. Near the door I caught a whiff of a scent, the cloying scent of musk oil. So one of my intruders had been Devin Ballantine!

Well, that did it. That was the last straw. I was

outraged that Devin Ballantine would dare come into my room uninvited.

Seething with anger, I pushed the chair away and unlocked the hall door. I hurried down the hall, past the staircase that ascended to the darkened great-room above, and scurried around the corner to Devin's door. Not wanting to wake up the entire household, I tapped lightly and called his name. When he didn't answer, I opened the door and went inside.

His room was at the front of the house. Light from a street lamp shone through the open shades to reveal an empty room. The bed was made. Devin had not retired for the night.

He wasn't here because he was out on the beach, one of those two people who were running up the beach.

I went back to my room, checked it again, locked it again, and finally succumbed to a restless sleep.

SIXTEEN

"I DIDN'T SLEEP WELL last night," Melanie complained on Thursday morning.

"Neither did I," I said. "What are you doing up so early?"

Melanie is the only woman I know who looks good in the morning, whether she's had a good night's sleep or not. She was wearing a sleep tee shirt that came down to her thighs, peach with green sequined apples stenciled over each breast. The caption read "Forbidden Fruit."

"I have clients looking at Gordon Cushman's house this morning," she replied as she padded across the kitchen barefoot and poured herself another cup of coffee. "And a new listing to get on the MLS this afternoon." For all her frivolity when it came to men, Melanie was a serious business woman, a billion dollar producer who sold residential and commercial properties. She worked hard even on vacation.

"Did you hear noises last night?" she asked me.

"I thought I heard sounds but they could have come from the street."

"What about Mickey? Did the noises bother him too?" I asked.

"Mickey? Well, ummmm, we had a little spat. Just a lover's quarrel. Mickey—oh, this is so silly—Mickey is jealous of Spunky." She giggled. "Men. Silly but still he got all huffy because Spunky sleeps with me—you know how possessive men can get. Says I love that cat more than him. So he slouched off to sleep in one of the guest bedrooms." She giggled again and examined her nail polish for chips.

"Yes, I've noticed that he's moody," I commented. So Mickey had slept alone last night and therefore had no alibi. But what in the world would Mickey and Devin have wanted in my room? I asked myself. And then to go chasing off down the beach? I shook my head in disbelief.

Melanie saw my reaction and misinterpreted it. "Men!" she said, arching her eyebrows. "Go figure."

I decided to tell her what had happened. "We had intruders in the house last night, Mel. Two people came into my room. They scuffled, then they ran out and left by the lower deck. That's what you heard."

She gave me a long look over the white coffee mug. "What? You must have been dreaming."

"If only. I had a bad night and couldn't sleep. I was out in the sitting room lying on the sofa so they didn't see me when they broke into my bedroom. Well, they didn't exactly break in. The door wasn't locked. They went into my bedroom, looked for something, then started fighting," I repeated.

"I don't believe it. Why didn't you scream?"

"I didn't know who they were. They could have been very dangerous burglars. They could have hurt me, Mel. I waited until they were gone, then I looked around. Now listen to this. One of the people was Devin."

"Devin? Ashley, I don't know what is going on but why would Devin sneak into your room with another person? That just doesn't make sense. I think you were dreaming. Is anything missing? Was something stolen? Let's search the house."

"No. Nothing was taken. But I know what I know. Devin Ballantine came into my room last night. You know that awful musk oil he wears? I smelled it near my door." I was hurt. She didn't believe me.

"Well, for pity sakes, lots of people wear musk. Could have been anyone. Oh I know, this is what happened: Devin came in late, maybe had too much to drink, and opened your door by mistake. And then you dreamed the rest."

I turned to leave, then warned, "I'm getting dressed for work. But when I get my hands on that Devin Ballantine, watch out. The feathers are going to fly, and they won't me mine!"

Feelings hurt, I flounced toward the stairs, a regular drama queen. "Maybe I ought to move back to my house where people don't sneak into my room at night."

Melanie followed me, an expression of disappointment on her face. "No, shug, don't do that. Please. I need you here. You're family. Are you coming back for dinner? Kelly and I thought we'd have a girls' night out. And we want you to come with us."

KELLY, MELANIE AND I were shown to a table out on the deck at Bluewater Restaurant. Kelly had on dark glasses and her hair was piled up under a baseball cap, in disguise but still heads turned and people stopped talking. She and Melanie made a really striking pair, one red head, one platinum blonde, both long-legged in their shorts. I had felt like a fifth wheel around them when we were growing up and for a second I experienced *déjà vu*. But I was no longer a child, I reminded myself.

The weather was perfect, warm but a soft breeze coming off the waterway. The deck adjoined a boardwalk where yachts tied up. "I'm going to get me one of those," Kelly said, pointing.

That reminded me of Devin and his story that he was here to buy a boat. "Why does Devin keep saying he's shopping for a boat but he never does anything about it?" I asked.

Melanie and Kelly both gave me an odd stare but kept right on talking about yachts. It was the way they used to treat me when they were in high school and I was in grade school—rendered me invisible.

"Hey, guys, I'm not a little kid any more. I mean it. What does Devin do for a living? Anybody know? Every time I ask him, he just changes the subject. He's evasive." Just like his brother, I wanted to say, but didn't.

Kelly had her face buried in the menu, hiding, when the waiter came to take our drink orders. Melanie ordered giant sized margaritas that came in goblets the size of soup bowls for herself and Kelly.

"I'll have iced tea," I said.

Devin had not been at the house when I got home from work. Neither had Mickey. Melanie said she'd been showing houses all day and assumed they were together because Mickey's car was gone.

I gazed across the waterway to the Bridge Tender Restaurant where folks were also dining out on the deck and gazing across the waterway at us. Airlie Road with its huge live oak trees and set-back fine homes bordered the waterway on the mainland side. In the blue water, stunning white yachts lay at anchor. A breeze rippled the water's surface; a sea gull flew overhead and squealed a hello. This was glorious, as good as it gets, I thought.

And suddenly I was resentful. Why was I sitting here in this glorious place, on this glorious summer evening with my sister and her friend when I had a perfectly good husband who would not stay at home with me? Right now I was as mad as hell at men. At Nick for being away and not returning my calls. At Devin for sneaking into my room. At Mickey, well just on general principal. He was bad news. Mad at all men. Even Jon was acting weird.

We'd put in a good morning's work at Kelly's house and at lunch time had taken a break and drove down to the riverfront for lunch at Elijah's. On the drive there I told him about the intruders in my bedroom and that I suspected one was Devin.

He was as stymied as I was about why anyone would come snooping in my room. "I hope you're locking your door," he said as he parked the SUV. "I think you ought to move back home. I don't like Devin and I like Mickey less."

"Melanie got upset when I suggested it, but I've

decided to cut my stay short and move back home on Sunday."

"Good, because otherwise I'm about ready to set up camp in your sitting room and sleep on your sofa. So, moving back home, that's the sensible thing to do," he said as we crossed Elijah's deck to take seats under a big green umbrella where we could watch the occasional barge float downriver. Our food came quickly and I munched on a char grilled burger. Heaven. A treat after all the seafood I'd been eating. Sometimes a girl just needs beef!

Jon was not himself, was quiet and brooding. Usually he's upbeat, a fun companion, an easy conversationalist. Then after consuming a fried oyster sandwich and downing a large beer he seemed to revive.

"Willie told me about the accident yesterday," he said as we waited for the check.

"It was nothing," I said. "The brick missed me. We've had worse near-misses at other restoration sites. What I don't understand is that I was sure I saw someone at an upstairs window. I thought it was you. But there was no one in the house when we searched. And where were you, by the way?"

"Having a late breakfast with Tiffany. No, don't get that look. I met her for breakfast. It was the only time she could take a break from shooting." Tiffany was an actress on a locally produced TV series. "I broke it off with her," Jon said soberly.

"But Jon, why?"

"Women!" he snapped and pushed back his chair. "Look Ashley, I want you to be careful. I don't want anything happening to my…partner." He wadded up his napkin, threw it on the table, and stood up. "Where's our check?" he demanded. He was in a snit, so uncharacteristic for laid-back Jon.

Kelly's muffled voice brought me back to the present. With the menu in front of her face, she was telling the waiter, "I'll have the crab cakes."

"Good choice," he responded.

"And a second round of margaritas," Melanie said.

Must be hard being a celebrity, I realized. Always hiding behind large dark glasses, or menus.

After he left with our orders—seafood lasagna for me and grilled tuna for Melanie—Kelly sipped her margarita then said to Melanie. "Ashley's right. What does Devin do for a living? And what about Mickey? You said he had a club downtown but I've never seen it and he's always hanging around the beach house."

"They had a broken water pipe at the club so it's closed for repairs. That's probably where he and Devin are right now. And I think Devin is a lawyer."

"Get out!" I exclaimed. "A lawyer!" Well, I'll be

doggone. Couldn't be. "I'd have thought ballroom dance instructor or cruise ship social director. With that heavy musk scent and those silky tropical shirts, he's like a throwback to a Dudley Moore movie. All he needs are gold chains around his neck."

Melanie laughed. The margaritas had lightened the mood. Maybe this "girls night out" wasn't such a bad idea after all. "Well, hey, don't hold back, shug," she giggled. "Tell us exactly how you feel about him."

Kelly confided, "I will say this about Devin, he has a real heavy-duty kind of friend. This guy came to the beach house several times this week to pick him up. Military type, the hair cut, the walk, the take-no-prisoners attitude. And driving a Marine Humvee. I mean a real Humvee, not one of those Hummers the pretend soldiers drive around on the interstate." She laughed. "He actually called me ma'am."

"Devin did tell me he had a friend who was a civilian contractor at Lejeune," I said.

"I'll ask Mickey about it," Melanie said.

"Well, I sure wish he'd lay off me," I groaned.

"Listen, shug, I've been meaning to tell you," Melanie began, "after Labor Day I'm going back to New York with Kelly for about a week. I need a break, and the market slacks off a bit right after Labor Day."

"We'll have a ball," Kelly said, and winked at Melanie. "The men aren't as cute in New York as our Southern boys but they are better dressed. I'll introduce you around. It'll be fun."

"And," Melanie said, turning to me, "I've never been to a Christie's auction before so Kelly and I plan to attend J.C.'s auction. And there will be parties with the big time art collectors. I can't wait."

I was thoughtful for a moment. "Remember how much fun we used to have when I was at Parsons and you and Mama came up for a visit. You'd stay with Babe and Ted and all of us would go out on the town. Those were great days. Gosh, I miss Mama."

"I miss your mama too," Kelly said, pulling off the ball cap and shaking out her hair. "I can't stand that thing another minute. Your mama was so cute with her *Gone With the Wind* stuff."

"I know!" Melanie squealed. "Let's drive down to Savannah for Labor Day and see her and Aunt Ruby. We can even invite Binkie." She turned to Kelly. "Binkie is Aunt Ruby's old beau from childhood, and I think they are rekindling the flame. Talk about cute, those two take the cake."

"That's a great idea, Mel. But Kelly, I've got to warn you, Mama probably won't remember you. She's changed a great deal."

"Yeah," Melanie said softly, and we all got quiet.

The sun was setting, the air cooling, and I was feeling mellow. Then I spotted Gordon Cushman heading our way and I groaned.

"What?" Melanie asked, turning her head. "Oh, hey, Gordon, pull up a chair."

Gordon lowered himself gingerly into the fourth chair.

I took a good look at him and did a double take. His cheek was bruised, he had a black eye, and his nose was puffy.

"Gordon! What happened to your face?" I exclaimed.

He tried to smile but it was more like a grimace. "You should see the other guy," he quipped.

SEVENTEEN

I'D DRIVEN MY VAN to the restaurant so after we finished dinner and drinks, I offered to shop for groceries for breakfast, and told Melanie I had to stop at CVS to pick up something. Back at the beach house, I put away my purchases then went out on the beach for a walk. It was only nine thirty, there was still an afterglow from the sunset and others were out for a last stroll. I had to get away from the house for a while and think.

My cell phone was in my shorts pocket. I never leave home without it. At night I set it in the charger on the bedside table. I carry it into the bathroom with me while I shower. It is always nearby. Often it rings, but the caller is never Nick.

Gordon Cushman had been in a fight—he never did give us the details—and last night I'd heard a fight in my bedroom between the two intruders. How much of a coincidence was that?

So was I wrong to think that my intruders had been the brothers grim, Devin and Mickey? Perhaps

Gordon Cushman had somehow gotten into the house, entered my room with Devin close behind. But how would Gordon know which room was mine? Well, he'd been a guest in the house before. He could have wandered around on the middle floor, checked out guest rooms. He would have been able to identify my room by my clothes. Who else in the household had a pair of steel-toed construction boots in the bottom of her closet?

But what was he after? Why enter my room? What did I have that Gordon Cushman could possibly want? And then I knew. Cushman was a collector and a dealer. And everyone knew that I had bought one of J.C. Lauder's watercolors only last week. Was Gordon looking for the picture in order to steal it? Then he'd sell it to one of those collectors who will buy hot paintings, hoard them, lock them away for private viewing. One of my classes at Parsons had included a session on stolen art works. And there were people like that, willing to keep their prize possessions a secret, as if the secrecy enhanced their pleasure.

So if Gordon was an art thief, had he stolen J.C.'s new painting from Valentine's gallery? Killed her for it? Then burned all the other paintings in that bonfire on the beach. We had only his word for it that he was trying to put out the fire. He could have started it, then put on a show for Jon and me.

It seemed hard to imagine Gordon killing anyone. He didn't have much in the way of testosterone. But how much courage did it take to pull a trigger? The gun did all the work.

And how did Devin fit in? Was he the middleman? The peddler of stolen art works? Devin a lawyer? It was hard to imagine. But then I thought of those *consiglieres* from the Godfather movies. Not all lawyers were honest.

J.C.'s paintings had gained tremendously in value. I'd paid a great deal for that small watercolor of the gazebo. But there was something about it, so fine, so controlled. You couldn't help loving it. And J.C. was a control freak if ever there was one. He must save all of his passion for his painting, I mused.

I had just about reached the Oceanic pier. At one time, Lumina, the renowned outdoor ballroom had stood on the site of the Oceanic Restaurant. During the days of the big bands, Lumina was the place where people from all around the state came to dance. Its hundreds of lights were doused during World War Two because of fears they might be seen by enemy ships at sea, and after the war they never seemed to burn as brightly again. Hurricanes and general deterioration led to Lumina being condemned, and although preservationists launched a valiant effort, the graceful old pavilion was demolished in the seventies.

On the pier outside the Oceanic Restaurant, diners were enjoying a late-night supper. Strings of lights from the outdoor dining area illuminated the beach where I marched along. After this walk, surely I'd be able to sleep. A large piece of driftwood had gotten snagged on one of the piles under the pier. As the tide washed in, the driftwood was carried higher on the beach. Then with the ebbing of the tide, the driftwood floated seaward only to get caught in the piling again.

Approaching along the water's edge, I became curious. That wasn't driftwood. The next time the wave washed out, I crossed the wet sand for a better look. And wished I hadn't. So this was where Devin Ballantine had disappeared to. If only someone else had found the missing Casanova.

I screamed for help and a number of people leaned over the pier's railing to ask what was wrong. I pointed and stammered and cried, "There! There!" When I pulled my cell phone out of my pocket and dialed 911, I was so choked up I could hardly speak.

EIGHTEEN

LATE ON FRIDAY MORNING, I was sipping coffee on the top deck with Officer Meriweather for company. The sun had already climbed high in the sky, the surfers were riding the waves, and two children raced around in circles on the sand while their mothers grabbed some rays. Serene, peaceful, cheerful—a normal morning at Wrightsville Beach. Amidst all this normalcy, last night's events seemed like a nightmare—someone else's nightmare.

But there was no denying it: Devin Ballantine was dead and I'd found his body. After the police arrived in full force, they made me wait out on the beach for hours. Melanie came, putting her arm around my shoulders, saying how dreadful. A drowning, a tragedy. Poor Devin. Poor Mickey. And Mickey came too and watched. He'd been like a statue carved in stone, very controlled and remote, a dangerous expression on his face, and I had expected an explosion. Melanie slipped her other arm around his waist but he shook her off.

More people came. A crowd formed. The word went around: a drowning. "Devin was a good swimmer," Mickey said, coming to life. "We grew up on the Jersey shore for Pete's sake," he added.

We stood there and watched the police set up flood lights, took backward steps when they told us, "Move back, folks!" and waited once again for the M.E. to arrive. Then it seemed like everyone staying on the island came out on the beach and assembled around the Oceanic pier.

"He must have gone out on the pier and fell off," Gordon Cushman said to no one in particular, and I turned around and saw him standing behind me, speculating like the rest of us.

"But there's a barricade," I argued, "and a 'Danger, No Trespassing' sign. Surely he wouldn't have gone out there. Everybody knows it's unsafe."

"That barricade wouldn't keep anyone off the pier if they wanted to go out," Melanie said in a low voice to me so that Mickey wouldn't hear her. "And you know what risk takers men are. They love taking chances."

"Undertow. It was undertow," J.C. Lauder said coolly and I swung around to see him there too, standing near Gordon Cushman. "Undertow is strong in these waters," he went on, lecturing the way he usually did. "Drags a swimmer out to where it's deep, then a few days later the tide carries the body back to shore. The trick is to not fight it, to swim parallel with the shore, but inexperienced swimmers don't know that. They struggle, swim against it. And that's useless. Undertow is too powerful, wins every time."

In the harsh light the police had set up, the body on the sand was clearly visible, no longer the sodden object I'd thought was driftwood but the distinct outline of a man.

Mickey, his hands balled up into fists, turned on J.C. "If you don't shut that smartass mouth of yours, I'm going to shut it for you." He took a threatening step toward J.C.

"That was his brother you're talking about," Melanie snapped. "Show a little respect."

J.C. gave us all a withering look, turned on his heel, and pushed his way through the crowd.

Everyone had come. Jon showed up later, and when he saw the horror on our faces, he put one arm around me and the other around Melanie and drew us to him, comforting us with the reassurance of his strong arms.

Everyone had been out on the beach last night. If Kelly had been there, I didn't see her.

"When was the last time you saw Devin Ballantine?" Officer Meriweather asked me, drawing me back to the pleasure of a gentle summer morning at Wrightsville. The children on the beach found a tide pool left by the surf and were splashing around in it.

Meriweather was questioning me as well as everyone in the house. He was about mid-fifties, solid, reliable. Fatherly. I'd been with Melanie a time or two when he'd issued her speeding tickets, that's how I knew him, and he had always seemed genuinely concerned about her safety and that her speeding would result in a serious accident. Not that it did any good. But I liked him, respected him.

"The last time I saw Devin Ballantine, Officer Meriweather, he was chasing down the beach with someone. That was late Wednesday night. I'm pretty sure it was Devin."

Meriweather gave me a searching but patient look that said: Take all the time you need but tell me about this. So I told him all about how two people had entered my bedroom while I'd been sleeping on the sofa in the sitting room.

"And you think the second person was Devin Ballantine? Why? Did you get a look at him?" Meriweather wiped a fine sheen of perspiration off his forehead with the back of his hand. The sun was climbing, relentless, it would be broiling hot soon.

"No," I replied, "but I smelled that musk oil he

always wore. It's cloying and strong and I can't stand the smell of it, so that's how I identified him."

Meriweather jotted a few notes in his note pad then asked, "Why would Ballantine come into your room at night? That part, I don't get. Was there something personal going on between you two?"

"What! No way!" I exclaimed, and realized the trap I'd set for myself. "Of course not. I don't know why he came into my room. I'm not even positive it was him, I just think it was. I think he followed someone else into my room, and the whole thing just puzzles me. What did they want? And why my room?"

"Did you bring anything valuable with you? Jewelry, for instance?"

"The only jewelry I've got with me is what I've got on: my wedding ring, my watch, diamond stud earrings. It's too hot for jewelry. All my other stuff is locked up at my house back in town, and I keep the alarm set."

"Okay, let's go back to the two figures you saw running down the beach. How do you know they were the same two people who entered your room? Why not a couple of boys horsing around on the beach?"

"I don't know. I just assumed the two figures were the same two people—men, I feel sure they were men—who had scuffled in my bedroom. I heard them go out on the deck below," and I motioned downward, "and they took the stairs down to the beach. It seemed reasonable that it was them. Besides, the two I saw on the beach were not horsing around. There was nothing playful about the way they were running. One was running to escape. The second, whom I assumed was Devin, was running to catch the first. Melanie heard noises that night too. Ask her what she heard. And Mickey was here too; he might have heard something."

"I'll talk to Ms. Wilkes again before I go. Mickey Ballantine isn't talking to us, by the way. But your sister told us that he hadn't seen Devin all day yesterday but wasn't concerned. 'He's a big boy,' she quoted him as saying. 'He can take care of himself.'

"Devin didn't have a car here," Meriweather went on, "not one that your sister knew about. Mickey had been driving him around, she said. But Devin could have asked for a ride from someone else, she supposed."

"That's correct. Devin didn't have a car here. I don't know how he got around. I've been working most days and didn't think about it. And Melanie has been working too so she wasn't here to keep tabs on him. But Kelly saw him go off in a Humvee with a friend of his from Lejeune."

"Hmmm. I'll look into that. I understand Devin

told Melanie he was shopping for a boat, so she figured a salesman had picked him up to take him to one of the marinas yesterday. Now we know different. The doc confirms that Ballantine had been dead for approximately twenty hours when you found him."

I lifted my coffee mug, then set it down, remembering. "Devin told all of us he was shopping for a boat, but I don't think he ever looked at one. He never talked about seeing one. Don't you think that if someone was buying something as special as a boat, he'd describe the boats he was considering?"

Meriweather didn't say what he thought. His noncommittal mask dropped into place. Then, as if choosing his words carefully, he said, "Now I know this is none of my business, Miss Wilkes, but I used to know your father. Your dad was a highly respected judge for New Hanover County. And you are married to a Wilmington PD lieutenant, and we all think a lot of Nick. So I can't help wondering why you and your sister are involved with a hood like Mickey Ballantine?"

"Involved! I'm not involved with anyone. Mickey is Melanie's friend, not mine. Besides, what has Mickey done?" I asked.

"Well, he's got a record for starters. Don't you girls know that? Armed robbery in New Jersey.

Served a prison sentence but got early release because the prisons were overcrowded. This is not the kind of man your father would want staying in your house. Your dad used to put away punks like Mickey Ballantine. As I said, it's none of my business, but I got a duty to protect you folks."

He was right. Daddy would be ashamed. I had never been comfortable with Mickey Ballantine.

"As I say, he's my sister's guest. I'll have a talk with her." I lifted my chin and looked him straight in the eye. He had a good face, a fatherly face. "I don't like him any better than you do," I said. "I'll tell Melanie I want him out of here."

"Good girl," Meriweather said.

"What did he steal?" I asked.

"He and some friends high-jacked a truckload of valuables: jewelry, antiques, paintings. They were part of an estate sale and being shipped to an auction house in New York."

"Auction house? You don't mean Christie's, do you?"

"Yes, I think that was the name. Why?"

"It's just kind of a coincidence. J.C. Lauder's collection is going to be sold at Christie's after Labor Day."

Meriweather grunted, then got up. "Thanks for your help, Miss Wilkes. You've given me a lot to go on. I'd like your permission to dust your bedroom and the doors for prints."

"Sure," I replied, standing up and straightening my tee shirt. I stuck out my hand. "I appreciate all you're doing, Officer Meriweather. I'll cooperate any way I can. Melanie too. I'll show you downstairs to my rooms, then I'm off to work."

Meriweather's handshake was firm and strong. "I'm counting on your cooperation, Miss Wilkes. Watch out for yourself, you hear."

"I will. Oh, and Officer Meriweather, I was wondering, what kind of work did Devin Ballantine do? He never said and no one else seemed to know."

"We're looking into his background, Miss Wilkes. Right now, I have no idea what he did for a living."

"But couldn't Mickey tell you," I asked.

"Mickey Ballantine is not cooperating. He's lawyered up. Makes me think he has something to hide."

"But surely you don't suspect Mickey of involvement in Devin's death. And anyway wasn't Devin's death an accident? Didn't he drown? Maybe fell off the pier."

"Sorry, but I'm not at liberty to talk about cause of death. You understand. Daughter of a judge. Married to a member of law enforcement." I led him back inside and down the stairs to my rooms as Melanie and Kelly watched, open mouthed. "Tell that husband of yours that Hank Meriweather sends his regards the next time you talk to him."

"Sure," I said. And I would. The next time I talked to him, but who knew when that would be. I was getting tired of waiting. I needed Nick here with me now. I called his cell phone number as I drove into town. When I got his voice mail, I said, "Call me right away. I've got important news to tell you."

NINETEEN

WORK ON THE LAUDER HOUSE was progressing smoothly. Kelly stopped by for a peek, but only a peek, because the subcontractors were at work all over the place. A foundation specialist was repairing the foundation, the electricians were working in the basement too and throughout the house. Plasterers were repairing wall and ceiling cracks, and a painter had started painting some of the trim work. The house smelled wonderfully of paint fumes and repair compounds even with all the windows open and large fans stirring the hot, humid air.

Sticking her head around a doorway, Kelly exclaimed, "Oh, my! The rooms look huge without all the furniture. It was always so crowded in here, Grandpa Joe saved everything. But now it looks spacious."

"The air-conditioning contractor says he can use the existing duct work so that makes our job much easier," I explained. "How you guys lived here without air-conditioning I can't fathom."

"It didn't seem so bad at the time," Kelly confessed. "We had fans set up in all the rooms, and took naps in the afternoon. I had a hammock in the backyard under that giant pecan tree and I'd take my English Lit books out there and read and doze."

She got a dreamy look on her face. "It was wonderful. Grandpa Joe knew I loved the house more than Uncle J.C. or mother. That's why he left it to me. Ashley, would this be a convenient time for us to go through the papers we left at your house? "

"Sure," I said. "Just let me tell Willie I'm taking off for an hour."

Since I'd been working downtown every day this week, I'd stop at my house at the end of the day to water the plants, go through the mail, and check the answering machine messages on the land line in the house.

Kelly saw the disappointed look on my face when I played back the messages and there was nothing from Nick.

"How long has it been since you heard from him?" she asked.

"Almost two weeks," I replied. "I'm frantic, Kelly."

"Oh poor Ashley. I'm so sorry. Isn't there someone else you can call?"

"I've called every person and number I know of. I've left messages for him at all those places. I just get indifferent replies saying that he'll call." I shook my head in frustration. "Oh let's talk about something else. Come on in the library. The boxes are there."

I showed her to my red library and left her to sort through the material in the boxes. "I'll be out on the porch watering my ferns. Holler if you want me."

I filled the watering can from the side spigot and watered my hanging ferns which were flourishing in the moist air. Some of the fronds reached the porch railing. I brushed my hand lightly over the soft fronds and murmured to the plants, one life form communicating encouragement to another.

Idly I sat in my wicker porch swing and watched as a few cars drove along Nun Street. Surely someone would have told me if Nick was injured, so I had to keep my spirits up and assume that he was well, just very, very preoccupied with—what? Translating documents? I go up wearily—my lower back had been hurting—and returned to the library where Kelly was pouring through one of the photograph albums.

"I should have shown these to Devin when I could." She turned her face upward to meet my gaze. "Ashley, I can't get over him drowning."

Nor could I. And Val getting shot. What was going on?

Kelly continued, "He was always asking about the POWs and here are pictures of them."

I sat down beside her on the leather sofa and we looked at the pictures together. They were the black and white snapshots from the forties with scalloped white edges. One picture showed six young men dressed similarly in work shirts and dark trousers. Under the photo, Peggy had penned their names in white ink: Eric Baden, Helmut Schultz, Claus Meese, Claude Schroeder, Karl Hoffwitz, Fritz von Loden.

Kelly said excitedly, "And look what I found among Great-grandfather's papers."

She handed me an official-looking document. "It's an application for citizenship," I said. "But it's blank, never filled out." We exchanged looks. "Do you suppose one of the prisoners wanted to stay and your great-grandfather was willing to sponsor him?"

"What else could it mean?" Kelly said. "I've been through the correspondence. Some of those prisoners corresponded with Grandpa Joe for years after they returned to Germany. They must have been very fond of him."

"How sad for everyone," I said, and flipped ahead through the album. "Oh look here's a snapshot of the gazebo in my painting." I motioned toward the wall where J.C.'s watercolor hung. "He must have painted that when he was a teenager."

I glanced at the painting on the wall again. "He

said it was one of the first things he ever painted. I just love it. There's such a strong sense of nostalgia about it."

"He's very talented, even as a boy," Kelly commented.

"You are born with that kind of talent," I said and turned a page. Two women in print dresses were photographed while standing in front of a flowering fruit tree. "And here's your grandmother Peggy with another woman. Is that your great-grandmother Marty? Peggy looks just like the portrait I saw of her on Tuesday."

Kelly looked over my shoulder. "Yes, that's Marty and Peggy."

In the picture Peggy was smiling broadly. "She looks happy in this picture yet you said she had a problem with depression."

"That picture must have been taken before all the trouble," Kelly explained. "Grandpa Joe said that Peggy had always been emotionally fragile, a shy girl. She kept to the farm. But then she met a soldier posted to Camp Davis. The soldiers used to roar into town on the weekends. There were dances at the USOs."

"The USO club at Second and Orange is still standing," I said.

"Anyway, Peggy fell in love. The soldier was

sent overseas and never returned. Peggy's heart was broken. And she was expecting. The truth is that was quite common in those days even if no one wants to admit it. They had such a double-standard back then. There were the 'good girls' and the 'bad girls' and girls from good families never wanted to be considered 'bad girls.'

"So poor Peggy faced this double whammy: she lost her lover, and she faced the stigma of an unwed pregnancy. When she and Uncle J.C. found William's body, that sent her over the edge. She was hopelessly depressed, barely functioning. After she gave birth to my mother, she was so dysfunctional Grandpa Joe and her doctors had no choice but to institutionalize her."

"This is such a sad story, Kelly," I remarked sympathetically.

"And it only gets worse. Because before Mother was a year old, Marty died of a heart condition. Grandpa Joe hired a housekeeper to look after Mother and Uncle J.C. who was ten at the time while he ran the family businesses. But he was devoted to the two of them. They were all that he had left of his family. And Peggy died in that mental hospital."

She looked like she was going to cry. "There wasn't a strong will to live in my family, was there?"

"Now, Kelly, don't say that. You and your mother and J.C. have turned all that around. And look at your great-grandfather; he lived to be ninety-four, and had you living with him when you were a teenager. I'd say the survival instinct runs pretty deep in your family."

Kelly smiled, reassured. "Yes, you're right. Trust you to put things into perspective, Ashley. You were always such a sweet little girl, following Melanie and me around. You wanted so much to be just like Melanie." She laughed. "Well, we all did. Melanie's something else. I love that girl."

"You're her best friend," I said.

"And Jon is yours."

I nodded my head.

"Lucky you to have a man for a best friend. Now if I could just store these boxes in one of your closets, then I'll move this stuff back into the house when it's finished."

"I've got lots of room in my suite at the beach house. Why don't we take them out there so you can get to them anytime you want to?"

"That'd be great, Ashley. More convenient."

We were both quiet and thoughtful as we carried the boxes out to my van and stowed them in the back.

I looked up and down Nun Street, seeing my

town differently, picturing it the way it must have looked during the boomtown war years.

TWENTY

WHEN I GOT HOME from work on Friday, I found Mickey in the greatroom, barefoot, dressed in shorts only. No shirt covered his chest but a lot of springy black hair did. A two-day old beard bristled on his chin. He looked liked he'd been sleeping all day and maybe he had. Owning a nightclub as he did, his days and nights might well be turned around. Officer Meriweather was right, this was certainly not the man Daddy would want for Melanie. I remembered my promise to ask Melanie to get rid of him, but there hadn't been time; she'd been working all day, so had I.

I almost said, "I see you're still here," but thought better of it. The man had just lost his brother. I mumbled a casual, "Hey," and took a bag of groceries into the kitchen and stored them in the refrigerator.

Mickey bent over the pool table and aimed the cue stick at the white cue ball, breaking the rack with such force the colored balls went caroming off into pockets or to the sides of the green field. He sauntered around the table, hunched over and fired another shot.

As he rubbed chalk over the cue stick tip, he said, "You'll be glad to know that as soon as the police release Devin's body, I'll be driving home to Atlantic City."

"Oh," I said, at a loss for words. He was right; I *was* glad. I was mindful of Officer Meriweather's warning that Mickey Ballantine was a dangerous man. The best thing he could do for Melanie was to stay in Atlantic City.

He didn't seem very upset by Devin's death, but then people grieve in different ways, and the hostility I was getting from him might have been a form of grief. I tried to put myself in his shoes, to imagine how I would feel if I lost Melanie. And I'd been raised to be courteous, to show respect for the bereaved. "Look, Mickey, I'm really sorry about Devin. What are the police saying? Was it a drowning?" Or foul play, I wanted to ask.

"I don't talk to the police," he said with an attitude and stalked around the table while holding the cue stick upright like a lance. "That's what I got a lawyer for."

Spunky appeared from out of nowhere and jumped

up on the pool table. "Scat!" Mickey hollered. "Be glad to be done with that cat," he growled.

But Spunky merely settled himself on the rim of the table and began to lick a white paw with intense concentration.

Picking up the thread of our conversation, Mickey continued, "The police talk to me through my lawyer. They said I shouldn't leave town, can you believe that? Not attend my own brother's funeral? Not be with my family at a time like this? My lawyer straightened them out but fast."

"Do you have any idea when they'll release the body?" I asked.

"Who knows? They're bringing in some hotshot investigator from the State Bureau. But as soon as they're through, my little brother will be on a train for home. My folks are taking this hard."

"I'm sure they need you. You ought to go to them," I said. And if an SBI agent had been called in, the police here must think it's a homicide, I realized.

"Yeah, but I can't go up there right now. Got business here I got to attend to."

"Uh huh," I said. Bet you do, I thought, as I moved to the refrigerator and poured myself a glass of iced tea. I returned to the pool table because I was curious. "Have the water pipes been fixed at your club?"

Mickey regarded me with narrowed eyes. "What? Oh, yeah, sure. They're fixed." He turned his back on me.

"This has to be hard on your parents," I said gently. "And you. If there's anything I can do, please just tell me."

Propping the cue stick against the table, he turned around and glared at me. If looks could kill! "Drop the phony-baloney, Ashley. I know what you think of me."

"Don't take this out on me, Mickey. It's not my fault that Devin drowned!" But wasn't it? If I had called the police when the men had intruded into my room, wouldn't they have intercepted them running down the beach? Wouldn't Devin be alive today?

I defended myself with, "This isn't about only you, Mickey. There's your family to think of. And Melanie. She's worried about you."

"Okay, since you're so nosy, this is what my lawyer says. Devin's death was no accident. They think he fell or was pushed off that pier. There was a blow to the head that didn't come from striking a pile. They can tell those things. But he did fall. And he did have water in his lungs—ocean water."

Picking up the stick, he turned back to the table. "Devin had more sense than to go out on that pier.

My mother didn't raise no stupid babies. Place looks like a good stiff wind would blow it in the ocean. But he would have gone out on a boat with someone. The wrong person."

"Have you talked to his friend?" I asked.

"What friend?"

"The civilian contractor from Lejeune. His friend. They spent time together."

"I don't know who you're talking about. Devin had no friend here."

"But he did. He told me. And Kelly saw him go off with this guy. A military type. Drove a Marine Humvee."

Mickey shook his head like I was hallucinating. "I'll tell you one thing, Ashley. Dev had the hots for you." He swept a critical gaze over my work clothes— a faded denim shirt, my khaki shorts, the pockets loaded with small tools. I was dusty and sweaty.

"Can't imagine why," Mickey continued and managed a mirthless chuckle. "But you wouldn't give him the time of day. Too stuck up."

"I'm married, Mickey, in case you've forgotten."

He seemed to ignore me then. Resumed his game as Spunky watched from his perch on the rim of the table, his head swinging back and forth to follow the action. Every time a billiard ball came rolling his way, he reached out to swat at it.

I was growing angrier by the minute.

"Take Melanie," Mickey said. "Now there's one beautiful dish. And Kelly too. They know how to look and act like women."

He stood his pool stick on the floor. "You know, you wouldn't be so bad if you'd put on some girly clothes."

I felt my temper flare and realized it had been close to the boiling point a lot recently. "Let's switch the subject back to where it belongs, Mickey, to your dead brother, not my clothes! Devin came on too strong. I'm married and very much in love with my husband."

"Yeah, sure. That's why you and Jon are as thick as blood. And where is the great detective? Melanie said you've been eating your heart out because he's not calling you."

Oh Melanie, I thought, disappointed, why do you have to tell my secrets?

Mickey picked up the cue stick and turning to the table shot the cue ball so hard it bounced. "Anyways, Devin didn't mean no harm by flirting with you. He was a good guy. Too good for his own good."

"And what is that supposed to mean, pray tell?" I asked sarcastically.

"Just what I said. Too good for his own good.

Always wanting to go his own way, not like the rest of the family. Joined the Army right out of high school. My old man went ballistic."

"But Devin told me he worked his way through college," I said remembering our conversation of one week ago, when he'd behaved like a decent sort of guy, before he started acting like Junior Jerkman.

"He did. But that came later. He was the only one in the family to get a college degree. See what I mean, Ashley. I tried to get him to go in with me on the nightclub and my other business interests here but he had to do things his way. I made him a good offer too."

He looked at me for my reaction but I took a long swallow of iced tea, thinking. Meriweather had said that Mickey and some of his friends had been convicted of armed robbery. I wondered if Devin had been in on that. Then later Mickey had tried to get Devin to join him in his nefarious underworld activities here in Wilmington. But Devin wanted to do his own thing. And what was that? I wondered. If Mickey trafficked in stolen paintings, was that Devin's line of work as well?

When Melanie, Kelly, Jon, and I had returned to the house after finding Valentine's body, Mickey and Devin were already here. Their luggage had been piled up against the wall.

I looked at the blank white wall where the luggage had stood, seeing it again.

But what time had they arrived on the island? Had they been here all morning? Time enough to kill Valentine, take J.C.'s painting and all the others, hide them somewhere, maybe in Mickey's Ford Bronco, and act innocent when we showed up.

Then when they discovered the other paintings were worthless, they set fire to them out on the beach and fled. Not being from around here, they wouldn't have known about our ordinance prohibiting open fires on the island. I recalled how Devin had disappeared from the bonfire site before Meriweather arrived.

Had Mickey and Devin argued over the painting, quarreled over how to split the money they would get when they sold it to a private collector? Thinking back, I had been working all that day and so had Melanie. I didn't know what Mickey and Devin had been doing. They could have been fencing the painting on any one of those days. Perhaps their quarrel over money had taken a nasty turn, so that Mickey clubbed Devin and threw him off the pier.

Devin had been in my bedroom on Wednesday night, the night he died. Then he'd chased someone down the beach. Or that's the way I assumed it had happened. Maybe he wasn't the one doing the chasing, but the one being chased.

I couldn't help thinking again that I should have called the police that night. But I had been desperate for sleep. Still, I thought guiltily, if I had involved the police, Devin might be alive now.

"Whether you believe me or not," I said earnestly, "I'm sorry for what happened to Devin. No one deserves that."

I was shocked when Mickey grinned. "Oh, quite a few do, little girl. Quite a few."

He leaned over the table and sent the cue ball caroming into the 4-ball which went rolling straight for Spunky. The cat lunged for the ball, digging his claws into the green felt.

"Damned cat. Get out of here," Mickey yelled, raising the cue stick threateningly. "Made me miss my shot."

I darted forward and was about to yell at him to stop when I saw that Spunky was not at all afraid. He just gave Mickey a level, unblinking stare. His gleaming eyes seemed to say: You wouldn't dare hit me with that stick because you know if you do Melanie will throw you out of her bed, and out of her house.

Mickey seemed to have second thoughts about

taking on Melanie's cat. For now anyway, and with me there as a witness. He lifted Spunky off the table with one hand and set him gingerly on the floor. "Go away, kitty. Go find a mouse to torture."

Tail raised high to show that his dignity had been impugned, Spunky skulked off, a black creature in a sea of white. No place to hide in all this damned whiteness, he was probably thinking. I decided to keep an eye on him.

Mickey leaned a hip against the table and idly watched the cat go. "You should have given Devin a tumble while you had the chance. He would have been good for you, smoothed off your prickly edges. Women get bitchy when they've gone without sex for too long. Devin didn't mean no disrespect. Like I say, he was a good guy. All that talk was just an act. A front."

I put my empty glass into the dishwasher and headed for the stairs to my private suite where I'd lock the door and have a nice long shower, wash off the dirt from the site and from my encounter with Mickey Ballantine. "A front for what?" I asked over my shoulder.

But Mickey just threw down the cue stick and strode across the greatroom to the master suite. "Wouldn't you like to know," he said, getting in the last word before he slammed the door.

TWENTY-ONE

ON SATURDAY MORNING Melanie and I had breakfast on the top deck. From the next house, the piano player was practicing scales. Melanie had her feet up on a chair, painting her toenails a deep coppery brown. On the other side of the sliding glass doors, Spunky watched us, meowing pitifully.

Kelly had spent the night with a girlfriend in town and Mickey was sleeping in.

"I heard Mickey come in early this morning," I said. "Where does he go at night?"

"His kind of business takes place at night, Ashley," Melanie explained as if that was something everyone should know and understand. "He's going through a rough time as you can imagine. It helps him to keep busy."

Yes, I thought, but busy at what? "What does Mickey do, exactly?"

Melanie looked up at me, her eyes wide in astonishment. "Why, he runs a very successful nightclub. You know that. What's ailing you this morning?"

She set the bottle of nail polish on the table and got up to pad across to the closed sliding glass door. Pulling the door open a foot, she said, "Spunky, come on out. It's okay. Just stay on the deck."

Spunky placed a tentative white paw on the decking, then froze. Melanie bent down and picked him up. "Come on, silly cat. You can sit in my lap." Carrying the cat back to her chair, she sat down and placed Spunky in her lap. He settled his body on her legs but held his head high, ears twitching, alert to the gulls' shrill cries, to high-pitched children's voices coming from the beach, to the piano in the next house.

"Mickey doesn't like him," I said. "I'd keep an eye on Spunky when Mickey is around if I were you."

"Oh, shug, Mickey likes Spunky. That's just his way."

"Don't say I didn't warn you. Look, we've got to talk. Saturday is a work day for me so I'll be leaving soon. This driving back and forth, downtown and back again is getting inconvenient, Mel. I'm moving back to my house tomorrow. And I think you would be wise to ask Mickey to leave. People are starting to talk."

I had rehearsed this speech in the mirror while I'd done my hair and makeup. I detested Mickey and I refused to stay in the same house with him. I'd been so angry last night I scarcely slept. The nerve of that guy. My sex life was none of his business. And his indifference to Devin's death was more than I could comprehend. How does Melanie stand him? I wondered.

Melanie looked alarmed. "Oh no, shug, I've had this summer planned since spring. You, me, Kelly. If it's Mickey that's bothering you, he'll be gone in a few days." She shrugged bare shoulders. "And you know I don't give a hoot about what people say."

"Well you should. You've got a professional reputation to maintain. And his sleazy reputation is rubbing off on yours and mine. So while we may be rid of him for a few days, like a bad penny he'll turn up again."

"How can you be so callous?" she asked. "Mickey's in mourning."

Without warning Spunky leapt out of Melanie's lap, crossed the decking daintily and jumped up onto the railing. "Don't sit up there, you silly cat," Melanie called. "You'll fall."

"Cat's don't fall," I said. "Look he's enjoying the view."

"You're wrong, cat's do fall. But I'll let him sit there for a while. As soon as I finish my toenails,

I'm going back inside and taking him with me." She pouted. "You never like any of my boyfriends."

"I liked Cam. All the rest have been scuzzballs. You deserve better, Melanie. Why you dropped dear Cam Jordan is more than I can understand."

Cameron Jordan was the executive producer of a successful television show and the president of Gem Star Pictures which he founded. He was crazy about Melanie. Yet she had dropped him to take up with Mickey Ballantine, nightclub owner, ex-con.

"Oh, Cam was so staid and puritanical," she complained. She put the cap on the nail polish bottle.

"Well, we'd never accuse Mickey of being that," I said. "He has a prison record, did you know?"

Melanie got up and went to the railing to pick up Spunky. "Yes, and he was framed. He took the fall for someone else. Mickey is legit, Ashley. Prison was an excruciating experience for him. He'd never do anything to risk being sent back."

She started inside. I followed. Melanie had always been plagued with tunnel vision: she saw only what she wanted to see.

"What are your plans for dinner?" she asked cheerfully, as if the subject of Mickey leaving and my not staying had been settled.

"I haven't thought about it. Grab something

downtown with Jon, I suppose. I'll be back later. But tomorrow morning I'm moving back to my own house."

"Don't make a hasty decision. We'll talk about that later tonight. I'll be here when you get in. Mickey's grilling steaks, and we're having a quiet evening at home. Kelly is going to a party at her friend's downtown. We were invited too but under the circumstances, it wouldn't be appropriate for us to attend."

She started across the greatroom to the master suite, then stopped and turned. "I still can't believe it's true, shug. Devin was just so full of life and now he's gone. Dead. Gordon is saying the police don't believe it was an accident. But what else could have happened? This used to be such a safe place when we were growing up. But now, so many psychopaths running around. First Valentine, now Devin. Poor Mickey. Try to be nice to him, will you, Ashley. He's going through a rough time."

And then, I couldn't help it, I felt guilty. I stomped down the stairs to my rooms. Stop pulling my chain, Melanie, I wanted to scream.

Late Saturday night I could not sleep again, too much on my mind. Jon had had plans with a friend so we couldn't eat together. Wishing to avoid Mickey, I'd stayed downtown. Willie had invited me to his house where they were grilling barbecued ribs. So I went off to his house with him and ate with his wife, his sons, his grandsons, and what seemed like fifteen great-grandchildren.

I missed being a part of a family. I wanted my own.

TWENTY-TWO

I WAS THE FIRST ONE UP on Sunday morning and got the decaf coffee started. After it finished dripping, I carried a large white mug out onto the deck, and started laying my plans for the day. Pack up my belongings, explain once again to Melanie why I couldn't stay, then drive back to town. I'd stop at Harris Teeter on the way to pick up milk, cereal, bread, and fruit.

As I sipped coffee and watched the early morning strollers on the beach I reviewed the progress we were making on Kelly's house. Things were moving along smoothly and there had been no more falling bricks, no near misses.

The insistent ringing of the telephone from inside the greatroom brought me back to the present. I padded across the deck barefoot and entered the house.

"Aunt Ruby!" I exclaimed when I heard her voice.

"Ashley, dear, is Melanie there with you? I need to talk to both you girls."

"Is something wrong with Mama, Aunt Ruby?" I asked, and felt my heart begin to thump. I knew things could only get worse still I'd never be prepared for bad news about my mother.

"Go find Melanie, sweetheart. Tell her to pick up the extension. I have to talk to both my girls together."

I carried the phone with me to the master suite door, all the while begging Aunt Ruby to tell me what was wrong. I tapped on the door. Then tapped again. Melanie did not respond. Finally I opened the door.

Melanie was asleep. And very much alone. No Mickey. Had he gone down to his club late last night? Was he asleep in another room? Had she thrown him out? I hope, I hope, I hope.

"Melanie! Wake up!"

She lifted her head, squinting at me.

"It's Aunt Ruby. Something's wrong. She has to speak to both of us. Pick up the other phone."

Instantly, Melanie was wide awake. She sat straight up, eyes alert and very much awake. And grabbed up the bedside phone.

"Aunt Ruby! I'm here, me, Melanie. Ashley's about to have a conniption fit. What's wrong?"

I moved inside her bedroom and dropped down on the edge of the bed. Melanie's eyes held mine as we both listened to the news.

"My darling girls, I'm so sorry to have to tell you this, but your dear sweet mother has passed."

"No!" we cried together. We moved closer, our free hands clutching each other, squeezing, holding on to each other for dear life.

"It was a peaceful passing, my dears. She died peacefully in her sleep, the poor dear thing. The look on her face was…angelic. She's at peace now, girls, and in a better place. Remember that."

TWENTY-THREE

THE REST OF SUNDAY and Monday passed in a haze but certain events stood out. We met Aunt Ruby at the train station on Monday morning. The three of us cried openly there on the platform, and waited and watched while the undertakers removed Mama's casket and transferred it into the hearse. I'd always thought the day my father had died in a fatal car accident while swerving to avoid hitting a golden retriever was the saddest day of my life. But the sight of Mama's casket coming off that train would be seared in my brain as the icon of grief forever.

I don't remember what happened next. I have no memory of taking Aunt Ruby back to the beach house, or of getting her settled in one of the guest rooms, but surely that is what we did. If I ate, I have no memory of putting food or drink into my mouth, yet I must have.

I do remember trying to reach Nick. Repeated calls to his cell phone. Jon never left my side. As soon as he heard, he was with me. He tried to find

Nick for me by calling the Wilmington PD Chief and telling him there had been a death in the family and that it was urgent for us to reach Nick. The Chief gave Jon the telephone number he had for Nick but it turned out to be the same number we had, Nick's cell phone number.

The Chief said he would contact CIA headquarters himself and promised to get word to Nick. Hours later he called to report that although he had not spoken to Nick directly he had spoken to someone who assured him the message would be relayed to Nick. Where was he? Why wasn't he returning my calls? How could an assignment like translating cell phone "chatter" cause him to be so inaccessible?

There were people in the house, they came and went. I don't remember who they were, sympathetic faces that floated in and out. Jon took me for walks on the beach at sunset, held my hand, and didn't speak unless I spoke first. He saw to it that I had meals and rested.

Years ago Mama and Daddy had written their funeral instructions. As a lawyer and a judge, Daddy had first hand knowledge of the messes people made of their private affairs, and he'd had the foresight to plan for any contingency.

There would be no lavish funeral service, which

both Mama and Daddy had objected to on the grounds that a long, drawn out visitation followed by an emotional service were just too hard on the mourners. How many times had they heard tales of someone having a heart attack or a stroke at a funeral? They both had wanted a simple graveside service at Oakdale Cemetery. No viewing! They had been adamant about that. I once recalled Daddy jokingly saying that he would sooner have strangers look at his naked body than his dead body!

And that was fine with me. I wanted my last image of my parents to be of them as living beings.

The service was scheduled for four, the hottest hour of the day, and Tuesday was a scorcher even in the morning. Melanie decided she didn't have anything to wear that was somber but cool and had to shop.

I hadn't given any thought to what I would wear, I was in such a stupor. I'd probably have put on shorts and a tee shirt as usual unless someone stopped me.

Melanie and Kelly laid down the law about that and so late Tuesday morning, they dragged me to Lumina Station. Besides, they said, I needed to get out of the house. Only those two would think of clothes at a time like this but they said we needed appropriate clothing for the funeral, lightweight but dark in color, something simple yet chic. I swear, that is exactly what they said.

Yet I know that Melanie was as devastated as I was by Mama's death. As her best friend Kelly was being excessively supportive and doing whatever she thought would help Melanie cope. And if that was a shopping trip, so be it.

Aunt Ruby was invited but she explained that Binkie was coming and they were going to have iced tea out on the deck. "At my age I attend so many funerals, I have a funeral dress for every season. But you girls run along and try to keep your spirits up."

We left her in her room, applying lipstick and blush with Spunky sitting upright at her feet, watching every move. The watch cat on duty!

"She's a tower of strength," Kelly said as we got into Melanie's Jaguar. "You're lucky to have her. My mom has always been kind of frail and Dad and I have to look out for her."

As Melanie drove up Waynick Boulevard toward the bridge at a remarkably noticeable leisurely speed, she said, "But your mom left home at eighteen and had a fabulous modeling career in New York. That took courage."

"My mom's career is one of those success stories you read about. She was studying fashion design in

New York when the famous model agent Eileen Ford saw her on the street. She stopped Mom and pressed her card in her hand and insisted she come in to see her. Mom thought it was some kind of joke and was about to throw the card away when her friends had a fit. They herded her into the Ford Agency *tout de suite*.

"Mom modeled with Twiggy—I've seen pictures of her, what a bean pole; and those false eyelashes, but that was the style in the sixties—and Lauren Hutton. Mom lived at the Barbizon Hotel for Women, the very 'in' place for nice girls in those days, and hung out at Studio 54. That's where she met Dad. He was in advertising, a young account executive."

"Your mother is still a beautiful woman," Melanie said as we touched down on the mainland.

"Yes, but there's always been that sadness about her."

I didn't say anything but thought that both our mothers were not typical moms, if there was such a thing. I wondered what kind of mother I would make when my turn came. Mama had always been so other-worldly, so lost in the fiction of the Old South. In many ways Melanie had raised me.

We pulled into Lumina Station, and even its verandas and fountains did nothing to dispel the sultry heat. Melanie headed straight for R. Bryan Collections. "I know we'll find the right things there."

I slouched along behind them, not interested in clothes, not interested in anything. Once inside Melanie seemed to lose heart, became all fluttery and couldn't make a decision, fell into a chair. Kelly did most of the work and was able to find us outfits in thin linen, chocolate brown for Melanie, navy for me, black for herself. And large straw hats in matching colors to shade us from the sun. She drew out a credit card and paid for everything.

"Shug, you look pale," Melanie said, peering into my face. "Doesn't she look pale, Kelly? Let's get some food into her."

We walked to Fathoms Bistro a few doors down. A party of brave souls was sitting outside at the swinging table. "Inside," Melanie told the hostess, "where it's cool. And have someone bring us sweet iced tea right away. My sister's not feeling well."

When the iced tea arrived at our table, she said, "Drink that now, Ashley. You look peaked. The caffeine and sugar will do you good."

She turned to Kelly and said, "Ashley's usually so strong, but Mama's death has hit her hard."

"Why are ya'll talking about me like I'm not here?" I asked bitterly.

"Sorry, shug," Melanie said sweetly, "you feeling any better?"

"Yes, actually, I am."

Then I smiled at her because she was so worried about me and coping with her own grief as well. While we waited for our sandwiches, we reminisced about Mama and Daddy. "Remember how we made homemade ice cream?" I asked and Melanie nodded, looking as dreamy as I felt.

For a moment I was transported back to childhood. On hot summer afternoons, we made ice cream in our shady garden, cooled by breezes off the waterway that rustled the centuries-old live oaks. Melanie and I took turns helping Daddy turn the hand crank, which became less and less yielding as the ice cream hardened, while Mama scooped handfuls of ice cubes into the stainless steel canister. At memories like this, I missed my parents so much the loss felt like a knife slicing through my gut. Daddy was the first to go, now Mama had joined him. I comforted myself by picturing their happy reunion in heaven, where I would join them again one day.

Impulsively I squeezed Melanie's hand, "We're the only ones left of our family. We've got to stick together, no matter what."

"I'll always be here for you, shug. I love you, little sister."

"Back at you, big sis."

We grinned.

Kelly clapped.

As we left the restaurant, I looked out into the parking lot and spotted Mickey in his Ford Bronco, parked off to the side in a shady spot. The windows were lowered and a man was in the passenger seat. I was about to point him out to Melanie who hadn't seen him yet but hesitated because it appeared that he and the other man were quarreling. The man was Gordon Cushman.

"Melanie, there's Mickey," I said.

She stopped and looked where I pointed. "Oh, he's with Gordon."

"Why does seeing those two together smell like trouble to me?" I asked her. Maybe it was the vibes she was giving off because clearly she was not going to approach them.

"I'll explain when we get in the car." And she trotted off with a sudden surge of energy.

With the air conditioner turned up full force, she backed out of the parking slot, and headed back toward the bridge. Even the watercraft on the ICW appeared sluggish as they skimmed the water at a snail's pace.

"Okay, what gives?" I asked.

"Gordon is signing over his Orange Street house

to Mickey. Naturally, he had to tell me because I'm handling the sale."

"I don't understand," I said. Kelly was in the backseat and didn't say a word. Maybe she already knew. Melanie told her everything.

"Gordon owes Mickey a lot of money. Gordon is a hopeless gambler. And well…he lost a lot of money to Mickey."

"Lost money? How?"

Melanie put on her signal—very unlike her—and turned right onto Waynick Boulevard. "You don't want to know the details. I don't want to know the details. I told Mickey not to tell me. What I don't know I can't be asked to tell."

"Asked to tell by whom? The police? Oh, I see. So all the rumors about Mickey are true. Melanie, you've got to dump that guy! He's trouble with a capital T."

She reached over and patted my hand. "I know, shug. And I am. He'll be staying through Mama's funeral and then until Thursday. Devin's body was released by the police and the funeral is in Atlantic City on Friday. We've agreed that when Mickey returns to Wilmington, he'll be moving back into his apartment over the club."

I let out a long sigh. One ray of sunshine on the dismal horizon.

"So if Gordon's so desperate for money do you think he's the one who stole J.C.'s painting and killed Val? They say his fingerprints were all over the place and he even admits to being there that morning."

"Why don't they just arrest the guy?" Kelly asked from the backseat.

"Jon says the police do not have the weapon. And they don't have a witness. So not enough evidence to charge him."

But something in the case might break, I told myself.

TWENTY-FOUR

OAKDALE CEMETERY was as pretty as a park, a beautiful Victorian garden, with spreading dogwoods and tall, dense magnolias. It was not far from the Lauder family home in Carolina Heights and the residents there took strolls through the cemetery and used it like a park.

Everyone had been devastated when vandals desecrated the cemetery, toppling fragile Victorian tombstones and damaging statues. But restorationists and volunteers had been hard at work and signs of repair were visible.

Our funeral cortege wound along the parkway. Melanie and I and Aunt Ruby were in the back of a dark cool limousine, Aunt Ruby in the middle, Melanie and I on either side of her, clinging to her hands.

When we got out of the limousine we were escorted to chairs set up under a canopy. It was shady there but the afternoon was hot and sultry and there was scarcely a breath of air. The groups of townspeople who had known and loved my parents and had come to pay their respects wore hats and fanned themselves with handkerchiefs. In their suits and formal clothes they had to be very hot.

Directly in front of me stood the casket, so solid it looked like it could last for an eternity. Unlike the woman inside it.

There was a carpet of fake grass under my feet and I concentrated on it as Father Andrew offered the eulogy. Mama had been a long-time member of St. James Episcopal Church so that Father Andrew was able to speak about her from personal knowledge.

I heard only bits and pieces of what he had to say. I was feeling strange, out of it, lapsing in and out of reality so that at times I felt like I wasn't there at all. When Jon approached and took my elbow I knew it was time to get up and leave. I took a few steps to Mama's casket and placed a long-stemmed white rose on top of the blanket of flowers. "I love you, Mama," I whispered and began to weep.

Jon led me away. Vaguely I thought that it should have been Nick and then I realized that I'd stopped thinking about him. The present was just so overwhelming there wasn't room in my thoughts for anyone who was not here. People crowded around me, clucking and patting, uttering all the right words. J.C. Lauder approached me and related how he had known Mama when they were young. He had wanted to paint her but she never would agree.

Melanie and Aunt Ruby had gotten separated from me, lost among another group of mourners. I made the mistake of turning around to get one final glimpse of my mother's casket and saw that they were hastily lowering it into the ground.

My legs folded under me, the sky turned black, and the earth rose up to meet me.

When I came to I was lying in the backseat of the limo; Jon, Melanie and Aunt Ruby were on the facing seat. The air conditioner was turned high and the cold air helped. Through the windows I could see people staring, curious and concerned.

"Let's get her home," Jon snapped to the driver. The limousine pulled away from the curb and snaked around the cemetery parkways. Then we passed through the big open gates. No one uttered a word as we drove back to Wrightsville Beach.

Jon carried me into the house. Melanie and Aunt Ruby put me to bed. "She's usually so strong," Melanie told Aunt Ruby as they were closing my door. "She just hasn't been herself."

"We'll call a doctor," Aunt Ruby said.

"No!" I called from my bed. "No doctor. Just let me sleep a while. I'll be fine."

"Okay, shug," Melanie said and stepped back

inside my room. "Aunt Ruby and I have to attend the supper the members of St. Anne's Guild are putting on at the church. We simply must go. Mama was a member, you recall, and many people are expecting us. They'll understand why you aren't there. And Jon's outside in the sitting room. He'll stay with you."

"Okay," I whispered. "I just want to sleep."

She left and I felt myself dropping into a dark hole. In my mind I was descending into the crypt with my mother and for some reason it didn't feel too bad.

TWENTY-FIVE

WHEN I AWOKE darkness pressed against the windows. I remembered where I was and what had happened. I was starting to feel a little numb. The edge of grief was not quite as sharp as it had been, like a buffer zone had been erected between it and my emotions.

I got up and went to the bathroom, then sat on the bed and swallowed some of the sweet iced tea Melanie had left for me on the bedtable. Sighing deeply I turned off the light and settled back on the pillows, remembering my dream.

There was a soft knock and someone pushed my bedroom door open a crack. Light from the sitting room hit my eyes and I blinked.

"Ashley?" Jon called. "I thought I heard you moving around in here. May I come in?"

"Yes," I whispered. "Come in."

He came in quietly, shutting the door behind him so that only a faint outline glowed around it. Then he crossed over to sit on the edge of the bed. I reached for his hand.

"I need someone strong to hang onto," I murmured and started to cry. "I'm glad it's you and not Melanie. She's so worried about me, Jon. I keep feeling like I have to reassure her that I'm all right. With you I can let go, be myself. You're my best friend. You love me too."

"You don't know the half of it," he said softly. "I love you so much it hurts. I can't bear to see you like this, in pain. I want you like you usually are, feisty, ordering people around, putting them in their place." He chuckled lightly and stretched out beside me, on top of the blanket. "I need to hang onto you too, Ashley. You're the strongest woman I know. I admire you so much."

"Jon?"

"Ssshhh, just listen to me. Let me talk. There are things I need to say, things I could never tell you before. But now, here in the dark, maybe I can. It feels right."

"Jon…"

"It's always been you, Ashley, ever since you returned home from college and I met you all grown up. Before that you were just Melanie's little sister, a cute kid. And then you changed into a woman while my back was turned. You have no idea how beautiful you are. Oh, I know, Melanie has always stolen the spotlight, but you, you're beautiful in a quiet kind of way that takes my breath away. I can't get enough of looking at you.

"At first I couldn't tell you, didn't know how to make a move. We were working together. To you I was good old Jon, your work partner.

"Then you meet Nick and a blind man could have seen how hard you fell for him. It was too late for me. I lost you before I even had a chance."

"But what about Tiffany? What about your old girlfriend Christina?" I asked.

"Well, what else was I supposed to do? You were in love with Nick. I couldn't spend my life moping around. I had to move on, find someone else to take your place.

"But no one ever did. That's why those relationships never worked out for me. It was hopeless."

"Jon…" I yawned noisily. "We need to talk about this but not now. There's too much happening right now. I can't cope with anything else."

"I know this is not a good time. There never was a good time. I'm not asking anything from you, Ashley. Just that we go on being friends. I'm going to be the best friend you ever had."

"You are already," I said and smiled at him.

He sat up.

"Don't leave," I said. "Is everyone asleep?"

"Yes. And I'm not leaving. I'm just taking off my shoes."

He folded the blanket back and slipped in beside me. "I'm going to hold you. Here, put your head on my shoulder and go to sleep."

I snuggled close, felt his strong, solid body, smelled his good, clean smell through his clothes. He smelled like Jon, a very familiar and comfortable smell.

"Thank you for this," I whispered. "I don't want to be alone."

"You'll never be alone as long as I'm on this earth," he said.

TWENTY-SIX

A FLASH OF LIGHT woke me. Had someone opened the door then closed it? Melanie? Melanie come to check on me? And she'd find me with Jon. But she wouldn't think anything of it; Melanie was very open minded.

Jon was sleeping soundly, his arms wrapped around me tight. I wiggled free, looked at the digital bedside clock. Almost three a.m.

Then I heard a faint rustling sound. What was it? The sound of soft footsteps on the carpet?

"Melanie?" I sat up. At least my head was clear. I didn't feel groggy any more.

"What?" Jon woke up, startled. "Hey, you okay?" he asked and lifted his hand to stroke my back.

"Ssshh," I whispered. "I heard something."

Suddenly the room was bright with light. I blinked, blinded. Jon raised a hand to cover his eyes. "What…?"

J.C. Lauder was standing near the door, one hand

on the light switch. The other hand held a gun! Jon bolted from the bed. "Don't move!" J.C. cried. "Do only as I tell you." The gun was aimed at me. "I'll shoot her if you make one threatening move."

Jon raised his hands, palms open. "Take it easy, man. What are you doing here? What do you want?"

"Don't play coy with me! Now both of you, get up slowly. We're going for a little walk."

I never realized before that J.C.'s arrogant aristocratic looks were actually a cover-up for a cruel and savage expression. "But I'm not dressed," I protested. "I'm in my pajamas."

"That is of no consequence to me. Now get up, and get moving. You first, Campbell. Out into the sitting room, then we'll go out on the deck and down the stairs."

"Well, let me put on my shoes," Jon said.

He wasn't acting afraid at all. Should I follow his cue? Yes, I decided. Thank goodness my head was clear. It had been so hard to think with cotton wool wrapped around my brain.

"You don't need shoes," J.C. snapped. "We'll be on the sand. We're going for a little moonlight stroll to the Oceanic Pier. Should suit you two lovebirds just fine," he sneered. "And you acting so holier than thou, Ashley, but here you are with your husband away defending his country and you're snuggled under the covers with loverboy. A hypocrite like your mother. She thought she was too good for me."

"And she was!" I declared. "Don't you dare soil my mother's memory with your arrogant self-righteousness. You have no right!"

"Oh, don't I?" he chuckled evilly. "Okay, now loverboy, get a move on." He gave Jon a push with his foot. His balance and coordination were amazing for a man his age. Then I remembered seeing him practicing the yoga tree pose. He was an advanced yoga student. I had seen him practicing *asanas* out on his deck every morning.

Jon moved into the lighted sitting room but kept his pace slow. Was he stalling for time? The house was quiet, everyone asleep. What if I screamed?

"Hold out your hands," J.C. told Jon.

Jon did as instructed. J.C. pulled handcuffs out of his baggy trouser pockets.

"No!" Jon cried and stepped back.

"I told you I'd kill her and I meant it. I'm a crack shot. I'll shoot if I have to. I've got nothing to lose; I'm an old man. It's all or nothing."

Jon cooperated docilely. He gave me an almost imperceptible nod of his head. Was he sending me a message?

J.C. saw it. "No, she won't run. She's too smart for that. Because if she runs, you get it. Got it?" He laughed at his joke. And if I screamed for help, he'd shoot Jon. Oh, he had us all right. For a moment his back was to me as he handed the cuffs to Jon and instructed him to put them on his wrists.

The two of them stood between me and the door so I couldn't run past them and out into the hall for help. I could make it out onto the deck, but then J.C. would shoot Jon. And maybe shoot me as I ran. And would the police ever discover it was him? He was willing to risk it, take his chances. As he said, it was all or nothing. If he won, he'd sell his paintings at Christie's and be a multi-millionaire. If he lost, well as he'd pointed out, he had lived a full life.

I was standing near the white wicker glass-topped desk where a lamp glowed softly. On the desk lay the blue and green folder of the map of Wrightsville Beach that Kelly had left there. It was fanned out, flipped over to the Wrightsville Beach side, just as Kelly had left it. Quickly, I grabbed up a red marking pen and drew an arrow pointing to the Oceanic Pier. I whirled away from the desk.

J.C. snapped the cuffs on Jon's wrists, then turned to me. The map was behind me, my body blocking it from his view.

"Okay, now you."

I didn't argue, just slipped the second pair of handcuffs around my wrists. J.C. reached out and snapped them closed, reassuring himself that they were locked.

"Now we go down the outside stairs," he said.

Hot, humid air flowed in through the glass door when he slid it open.

"How did you get in the house?" I asked.

He chuckled. "Melanie's been handing out keys like they were party favors."

And he was right. How many sets of keys had Melanie distributed? Five that I knew of. It would have been easy to swipe a set.

"Now get a move on. Down the steps. Slow and easy. Hold onto the railing. I don't want you falling. And don't try any tricks, Campbell. I've got this gun aimed at the back of your girlfriend's head."

I followed Jon down the outside steps. We were barefoot but the wood had been sealed and it was smooth under my feet. I was very aware of the gun pointed at my head. I held onto the handrail with both hands and descended cautiously.

At the bottom, J.C. ordered, "Now cross over the boardwalk to the beach."

The boardwalk was lighted by a lamppost in the middle where the walk bridged the dunes. The moon sailed in and out of patches of dense clouds.

Once on the beach the ocean itself offered a glimmer of light.

The ocean was noisy, waves crashing, high tide was breaking and J.C. had to raise his voice to be heard. "Okay, you two walk in front. Step lively and head for the pier. And if you think you can outrun me, forget it."

Jon moved to my side and we started up the beach. "He means it," Jon said to me, "so let's do as he says. For now. But if you get a chance, run. Run as fast as you can to the first house you see."

"Stop that talking!" J.C. called from close behind us.

I inclined my head to let Jon know I had heard and understood.

We made our way north along the ocean's edge. Lights were out in houses, only lampposts remained aglow. White frothy waves pounded the strand and the clouds were a paler blue against the midnight blue sky. Even the sandpipers were asleep, perched on one leg, heads tucked under their wings.

I thought furiously, fear making me fully awake. Why was he doing this? Why were we a threat to him? He had to be the killer, the one behind the deaths. That was the only explanation for this bizarre behavior. Val's murder, Devin's drowning. But why? What had been his motive?

It was my room he had come to. And he knew which room was mine, so he'd been there before. My late night intruder? He had no way of knowing Jon would be there. Obviously it was I who posed some threat to him. But what?

My mind raced with possibilities. Had he wanted to steal his watercolor back from me? That didn't make sense. And was he the one who had stolen his painting from Valentine's gallery? Again why? For the insurance?

But that would mean he had killed Val, and they had been friends for decades. Then it came to me. He had staged the robbery of the other paintings as a cover-up. But why? It had to have something to do with his own picture.

Jon was staring at me intently. He had reached the same conclusion. And our deduction could only mean one thing. "He's going to kill us," Jon whispered to me.

J.C. didn't hear. The ocean's roar covered our whispers. "When I get a chance I'm going for him," Jon said. I lifted my hands in front of me, meaning how, how with the cuffs? Jon shook his head negatively. He didn't know but we'd watch for our chance.

The Oceanic Pier loomed ahead of us, stretching far out into the ocean. In the moonlight it looked like some sort of primeval beast, a multi-legged dinosaur with a humped back. We approached the pier and J.C. told us to stop. Foam tickled my ankles.

"Okay, up there. Up to the boardwalk."

Street lamps shone down on our slow procession but there was no one out. I prayed for a Wrightsville PD patrol cruiser out checking on things but none came by.

We crossed the sand to the Oceanic Restaurant. J.C. motioned us up the ramp that ran along the south wall of the restaurant. At the top of the ramp a tall gate barred our way. "It's locked," I said aloud, relieved.

But J.C. only sneered, "That rusty lock won't stop us." He lifted a foot and kicked the gate open, then chuckled, "The other night when I was here, it wasn't even locked."

The other night? I thought furiously. Oh my gosh, the night Devin drowned. He was confessing to Devin's drowning.

He steered us out on the pier, past the white plastic tables and chairs that were arranged under strings of lights. About a third of the way out on the pier, we came to the barricade with its "Danger" sign.

"Okay, squeeze through," he instructed. "Go ahead, there's plenty of room. I've done it, so can you." The spaces between the railings of the barricade were wide.

"J.C., take the handcuffs off," I pleaded. "I need my hands to balance me while I crawl through that opening."

"That's why I cuffed you in front. You've got the use of your hands. Now hurry up. You first, Campbell. Once you're out there, I know you aren't going anywhere." He laughed.

"You're crazy, Lauder. I'm not going out on that pier. It's about ready to collapse."

J.C. pressed the nuzzle of the gun against the back of my head. "Do as I say or I'll pull this trigger."

"Okay, okay!" Jon said and sat down on a cross rail. He swung his legs to the other side, then slid his upper body through.

"Now you," J.C. said, motioning with the gun.

I acted clumsy, stalling for time, pretended I couldn't do it. "I'm not as agile as you guys," I lied.

"Just do it!" he yelled and pressed the gun up under my chin to show me he meant business.

"Don't shoot her!" Jon yelled. "Here, Ashley, take my hands, I'll guide you through." He reached for me and I let him lead me, lifted my legs and climbed through the opening.

"Stand clear," J.C. ordered, "Give me room."

As sinewy and elastic as he was, he maneuvered through the opening in one motion. A flock of seagulls that were roosting on the pier let out raucous cries; angry that their sleep had been disturbed they flew up to circle the pier.

The pier was unsteady and swayed with our every movement. The decking undulated, buckled up then dropped down, like a roller coaster.

"Get moving," J.C. said, "down to the end."

The end of the pier was closed off by a few spindly railings, scarcely strong enough to hold the few gulls that settled there again.

Something sharp pierced my bare foot. "Ouch," I cried, and jumped on one foot.

"Steady, Ashley," Jon said, supporting me.

"It's just a splinter," J.C. said. "Stop being such a baby. Now walk down to the end!"

I hopped to keep my weight off my injured foot but my abrupt movements caused the pier to shift and I screamed. "Stop that!" J.C. yelled. I bent over again, trying to reach the sharp splinter with my cuffed hands.

Then I realized that in moving toward me to help me regain my balance, Jon had deliberately placed himself between J.C. and me. With his body blocking mine, he confronted J.C. "If you think I'm going to let you throw her off the end of this pier, you're nuttier than I thought."

I pressed up closer to Jon's back, making myself as small a target as possible.

J.C. waved the gun at us menacingly.

"Go ahead, shoot us now," Jon taunted. "That'd be better than a slow death by drowning. And who knows," he added, "maybe you'll miss. Maybe a cop car will come by and see us up here. Or a surfer will come out for a swim."

J.C. was growing angrier by the moment. "You think I won't shoot you?"

"Like you shot Valentine Russo," I accused. "Valentine! Who'd been your friend for decades, who helped you get established on the art scene. Are you going to shoot us like you shot her? She didn't even put up a fight. Why did you do it, J.C.?"

I wasn't able to see his face clearly but I visualized the sneer.

"She saw something she wasn't supposed to see. Meddling bitch. Then she had the nerve to call me and say, 'Hey J.C., we've got a little problem here. I'm mystified. There's something odd about this signature.'" He mimicked Valentine perfectly.

So that was it. The signature? Something was wrong with the signature. All of a sudden I understood. The signature was a forgery. And he thought I knew. That somehow I had found him out or maybe that Valentine had told me before she died. That had to be it.

He had turned away while he was talking, so

distracted by his anger, so outraged that someone had the gall to question the great J.C. Lauder that he dropped his defenses. Jon chose that moment to swing his cuffed hands at the back of J.C.'s neck. J.C. stumbled forward.

Quickly I jumped out from behind Jon and with my cobbled hands making a solid fist, I swung them so that the handcuffs clipped J.C. in the Adam's apple. He stumbled back, coughing, clawing at his neck. But he still held the gun in a solid grip and he raised his arm, pointed, got ready to shoot.

Suddenly, a third pair of hands intervened. A solo fist came flying from out of nowhere to hit J.C. squarely under the chin and send him flying. He staggered back but regained his balance and raised the gun to his assailant.

But Mickey was ready for him. He lunged at J.C. from the side, shoving him hard against the section of railing that bowed out over the ocean. The railing snapped like a matchstick. J.C. teetered for a second then fell off the pier with a loud scream. There was a thud sound and the pier shook badly as his body struck a pile directly beneath us.

Cautiously the three of us edged to the broken rail to look down. There was no sign of J.C. Then his body surfaced, buoyed by a wave. He was not struggling, not swimming, not moving. High tide carried him away from the pier. A huge wave rolled in, picked up his limp body and swept it out to sea.

"Undertow," Mickey said nastily. "Isn't that what he said caused Devin's drowning? Undertow."

TWENTY-SEVEN

THE NEXT DAY I SLEPT into the afternoon. We'd been up until dawn, while Officer Meriweather and a team of Wrightsville Beach's finest removed the handcuffs and listened to our story. A search for J.C. would commence at daybreak but there wasn't much hope of finding his body unless or until the ocean returned him to shore. My injured foot was treated and Jon and I were driven home.

Just as I was thinking it was time to get up—I was hungry; hadn't eaten in twenty-four hours—there was a tap on my door. "Ashley, come on out," Melanie called.

I forced myself to get up off the bed and open the door. Melanie looked so worried. "You've got to hang in there, shug," she said and reached out a hand to rub my upper arm.

"Listen," she continued, "Babe and Ted are here. So comb your hair and fix your face and come out and say hello. You'll want to hear what they have to say."

"They know something about what happened last night?"

"They have all the answers. Wait till you hear."

Hurriedly I splashed cold water on my face. Even so, my eyes were still red. Well, that was too bad! The world would just have to accept that I was in mourning. I ran a brush through my hair, impossible, but what could I do? Forget it, I told myself. This is the way you look. You've got the Wilkes family curls.

More tears flowed. I splashed more cold water. Managed a hit or miss with some lip gloss. Changed into a fresh colorful tee shirt. Then went upstairs to the greatroom. Melanie met me and handed me a mug of hot coffee.

"Is it decaf?" I asked.

When she said yes, I took it gratefully.

Babe and Ted sat side by side at the end of one of the immense white sofas. They got up when they saw me, crossed the room to my side, and enfolded me in their arms.

"We're so sorry, Ashley," they said together. They were so definitely a couple. A sting, like an arrow, pierced my heart. This is what I missed, this couple thing. Yet had I ever really had that with Nick? I wondered. Only for moments at a time.

Melanie took me by the hand and led me to the

other sofa. "Come on, let's all sit down. Mickey's fixing drinks. It's too hot to sit outside on the deck so we'll have our visit in here where it's cool. Come on, shug, over here next to me."

I settled onto the sectional where Melanie patted and sipped the hot coffee. "Where's Aunt Ruby?" I asked.

"Binkie came and got her and took her to see his house," Melanie replied and grinned. "I think there's romance in the air for those two."

Kelly came in from the kitchen with a tray of crackers and cheeses and sweet rolls for me, set them on the coffee table, then squeezed in between her parents. Absently, Babe stroked Kelly's hair. She looked just like Kelly, looked like her older sister, always had, looked very young for an almost sixty-year-old.

"It's my fault you were put in such a dangerous situation, Ashley. I'm so sorry. I never thought it would come to this," she murmured and I didn't know what she was talking about.

"We had no way of knowing they would send someone from the Judge Advocate General's staff down here," Ted said. "They didn't tell us what they were doing about the investigation."

"Judge Advocate General? Investigation?" I asked, confused.

Melanie couldn't restrain herself. "It was Devin. You won't believe it. Devin was a captain in the Army, a lawyer on the Judge Advocate General's staff. He was here doing some investigative work for them. That's why he behaved so strangely! He was trying to throw us off."

"No!" I exclaimed. "I suspected his drowning wasn't an accident. J.C. killed him too. But why?"

Mickey wheeled in the bar cart, used his left hand to pass out gin and tonics to everyone but me. His right hand was bandaged. He looked angry, but then that seemed to be his habitual expression. "I told you Devin was different," he said resentfully. "I told you he was too good for his own good. Now you know what I meant. And now you know why I helped J.C. off the pier when we had that scuffle. I shoved just a little too hard. I don't regret it."

I thought of sweet, kindly Valentine Russo. I didn't regret it either. But Devin? A lawyer? "Would someone please explain this to me? But first, Mickey, how did you find the map?"

Melanie interrupted. "You can thank Spunky for that. He heard noises and woke me, that smart little cat. Tapped my face with his paw until I awoke. Remembering how you said someone had been in your room the other night, I sent Mickey to investigate."

"And I found you gone," Mickey said, "and the

sliding glass door to the deck was open. Then I saw the arrow you'd drawn on the map and that really piqued my curiosity since that was where Devin had fallen. I hurried up the beach and saw you out there on the pier."

"Well, thank you, Mickey, you saved our lives."

"You are welcome, Ashley," he replied formally, "and I'm glad I could help you out but the truth is I was motivated by revenge."

"I can understand that," I said. "Okay, would someone please explain about Devin being a lawyer."

Ted began, "Babe and I contacted the JAG after we put two and two together. It never occurred to us that anyone here would be in danger. And they didn't confide in us about how they were conducting the case." He raised an open palm. "We knew nothing about Devin's role in any of this, Mickey, I swear."

"Nobody did," Mickey said, sitting down beside Melanie and taking her hand in his. "Not even me. I thought he was on vacation just like the rest of you thought. Sure I knew he handled investigations for the JAG but like I say I thought he was on vacation."

"But what was his role?" I asked. "Are you saying the JAG for the US Army was investigating the theft of J.C.'s painting? Why would they be interested in that?"

"Shush," Melanie said, "give them a chance to explain."

"They weren't interested in J.C.'s painting!" Ted declared.

"Weren't…"

"Let me begin at the beginning," Babe said. "Ted and I have had a lot of time on airplanes to piece this all together. The paintings were the clue, you see, including the clue to my origins. My mother was never in love with a serviceman who was killed in action, the way they said. That was just the story my family told to save face. My mother was in love with a POW who worked on her family's farm. I'm his daughter. I've got proof."

"What is it?" I asked.

"On our last trip here in the spring, I decided to clear out Grandpa Joe's personal papers and I found some letters."

Kelly interrupted. "They had been in the boxes we took to your house for safekeeping, Ashley. Only Mom had already removed the letters."

Babe continued, "The Schroeder family in Germany had corresponded with Grandpa Joe for years after the war. They were searching for their son who had been one of the POWs who worked on our family farm. Their son never returned home after the war when the rest of the German soldiers did. They included the last photo they had of him, a young man of about twenty. Well, I look just like him. Ted saw the resemblance at once.

"So I started writing to his family members who were left. Then Ted and I made the journey to Dusseldorf to see them. I met my father's family. My female cousins look enough like me to be my sisters. The young ones look just like you, Kelly. There were two aunts left, my father's sisters. My grandparents are gone, passed."

Ted drained his glass then continued the story. "The family had been writing to the US Army since nineteen forty-eight, inquiring about the whereabouts of their son, Claude. The last they knew he was a POW at the Old Marine Hospital camp here in Wilmington."

I leaned forward, staring at them intently. "Binkie told me and Devin about Wilmington's World War Two experiences with the POW camps."

Ted continued, "After Germany surrendered in May 1945, the POWs remained in Wilmington for another year. They weren't shipped back to Europe until April 1946. But since we were no longer at war with Germany, they were allowed to write home. That's how Claude's parents knew where he was. He told them he was in love with an American girl, that her father approved, and was applying for U.S.

citizenship for him. He'd never have run away. He said they were expecting a baby and that Peggy's father was happy about that. He told his family that if the U.S. government shipped him back to Europe, he'd go, but then he'd try to return to his new American family."

"But they weren't shipped directly back to Germany," I said, remembering what Binkie had told me. "There were war reparations to be made to England, and they worked the farms in England for another two years before they were allowed to return to Germany. But what do you mean the paintings are a clue?"

Babe explained, "I never gave those paintings a thought when I was a small child. They were just there, in the house, all around us. Pretty pictures." She smiled grimly. "I have to admit I was a miserable little tyke. No father, mother died in an institution. Grandpa Joe was good to me but he was a busy man, running the family farm and the store almost single-handed. Uncle J.C. made my life miserable."

She gave a shiver, remembering. "He was a sneaky, mean adolescent. He'd torment me when my grandfather or the housekeeper weren't around. Called me names like 'the little bastard' and 'the Nazi.' I was too young to know what a bastard was but I knew it was something bad, something to be ashamed of. When I went to school I learned exactly what it meant."

Kelly snuggled closer to her mother. "Oh, mother, I'm so sorry you had to go through that. What a bunch of small-minded hypocrites you had to contend with. And you an innocent child."

Babe shrugged. "Those were different times, honey. There was a double standard. But there were a lot of us, children born out of wedlock as it was commonly referred to. Other names, much worse. But most of the women managed to snag returning servicemen so their illegitimate children got stepfathers and some degree of respectability."

Melanie said, "So J.C. knew you were the POW's daughter. That's why he called you a Nazi. But explain about the paintings."

"Well, when I was about six, all the paintings disappeared. I didn't ask why. I was just starting school then, that was enough for me to handle. And that was about the time Uncle J.C. started painting. It was also about the time the farm was sold to developers who were building houses for GIs and their families. Now at the time, I didn't realize any of this. It has taken me a lifetime to remember the details and piece things together.

"Grandpa Joe must have given Uncle J.C. a share of the proceeds from the farm sale because as soon as he was eighteen he moved out and got his own place. And then later, he began selling the paintings, and he became very popular and started to make real money. J.C. was counting on me not to remember. And I probably wouldn't have if it hadn't been for finding that photo of my father. In retrospect, Grandpa Joe must have known, but what could he do? J.C. was his only living child."

"But if J.C.'s signature was forged, whose paintings are they?" I asked.

"Why, my father's," Babe replied simply. "According to his sisters, he was establishing himself as a fine artist when Hitler started the war and turned everyone's lives upside down."

Melanie jumped in, "And J.C. stole them, then passed them off as his own. He brought them out slowly, one every year or two."

"Exactly," Ted contributed. "And now I expect what's left of them belongs to Babe."

"So if that is what Devin and the JAG were investigating, I can see why J.C. got desperate," I said.

Mickey interjected, "No, Ashley, you've got it wrong. The paintings were merely a clue. Devin was looking into the possibility that Claude had been murdered. Why else would he disappear when Peggy's father was trying to arrange for his citizenship so he could marry her? Why would he abandon her? And why else would he leave the paintings behind? He was not listed on any of the departing ships' manifests? The Army kept good records."

"Oh," I interrupted. "Now I know why Devin spent time at Camp Lejeune with his civilian contractor friend. He must have been looking through the old Camp Davis records, trying to trace Claude."

Mickey continued, "Claude Schroeder never returned to Germany. That's because he never left the US! He's dead! History!"

"But Uncle J.C. was too young to have murdered anybody. He was only ten years older than me," Babe said.

"Wait a minute!" Kelly interjected. "Not J.C. It was William. I know something about this. Grandpa Joe was always talking about the past. He was in his nineties when I lived with him during high school. The past was so real to him, the way it is with old people. He reminisced about Peggy and William all the time, and his wife Marty. How Marty had worried so much when William was MIA that it ruined her health. About how changed William was when he returned home from the war. William hated all Germans. He blamed every one of them for the neglect he'd suffered when his plane was shot down and he was injured."

"So it was William who killed Claude!" Mickey declared.

Kelly moved to the edge of her seat, her elbows on her knees, her hands chopping the air excitedly. "That would explain why William hanged himself. I remember Grandpa Joe talking about that too. Peggy and J.C. were the ones who found him hanging from a rafter in the barn. The experience sent Peggy into an irreversible depression. It hardened J.C., made him mean. After Mother's birth, Peggy was so depressed she was dysfunctional and she never recovered. He told me that once when I asked him about her dying in an asylum. But it wasn't simple postpartum depression, it was losing Claude, then finding William's body. That was too much. She went insane."

"But you're saying that William killed Claude and J.C. knew," I said.

"Well, I never realized that before," Kelly said. "I always believed the story they handed Peggy, that Claude abandoned her. But now, I agree with Mickey, William killed Claude. Probably he couldn't stand the thought that a German had been his sister's lover, and that a baby was coming. He must have been in a blind rage. And J.C. either knew about it or was his accomplice."

"But where is the body?" Melanie asked.

"Why, I suppose it's buried out there somewhere on the farm property, covered over with streets, houses and lawns by now," Babe said.

A sudden insight caused me to gasp. "No, not there. I know where it is!"

TWENTY-EIGHT

I TELEPHONED JON and did my best to explain the scenario our group had pieced together. Jon called Officer Meriweather. Meriweather said he had to confirm things with the JAG's office and he'd get back to Jon.

An hour later Jon arrived at the beach house. "Meriweather and a few officers are going to meet us at the Lauder house. Since it's in Wilmington PD's jurisdiction, Detective Diane Sherwood is going to meet us there. Let's go."

Everyone jumped up.

"No, we can't all go. Just Ashley and me. You ready?" he asked me.

I was ready, had quickly showered and put on shorts and a tee shirt, sandals.

Ted followed us out. "Call us and let us know the outcome," he said, and we assured him we would.

As Jon drove away from the beach, I filled him in on the details, and we speculated about J.C.'s motives.

"He must have known he was a mediocre painter," I said.

"Kelly said he'd started taking art classes because he had been inspired by the drawings of one of the prisoners. That was just the story he told. I think he later realized he wasn't good enough. When hostilities ended with Germany, some of the pressure must have been off so that Babe's grandfather might have been able to get Claude posted to their house, or the farm, something like that. In two years time, Claude had produced dozens of paintings. Grandpa Joe had liked Claude and was willing to accept him as a son-in-law. He had started the paperwork to obtain citizenship for him."

Jon continued the thread. "Then after William killed Claude, William and J.C. hid his body, then told their father and Peggy that Claude had run away. Peggy would have felt abandoned and ashamed. Later, J.C. hid all the paintings until he was old enough to get his own place. Then, over the next fifty years or so, he brought them out one by one, claiming them as his own work. As Babe said, her grandfather must have known but what could he do? Expose the only child he had left as a fraud? And Babe was too young to think much about missing paintings when he removed them from the house."

I said, "While we were waiting for you to call with Meriweather's decision, Kelly and I went through the boxes we'd moved from my house to the beach house. We got a magnifying glass and studied the signature on the drawings Claude had made for Marty. The signature was faint but legible. 'CLAUDE' it read. No last name, just 'CLAUDE' in block letters, all caps.

"That's why J.C. entered my rooms that night. He was looking for those drawings but at that time they were at my house in town."

"And Devin must have been watching for something to happen, and so he followed J.C. into your bedroom."

I rubbed my arms. "Gives me the shivers."

"We're here," Jon said as he parked in front of the Lauder house behind two Wrightsville cruisers. "The similarity in names made it easy for J.C. He had only to put a period after the 'C' and prefix it with a 'J' then add an 'R' at the end of 'LAUDE.'"

"But eventually Val detected some irregularity with the signature. Maybe a difference in the paint, something. I wonder why she never saw a discrepancy before."

"We'll never know," Jon said. "Probably she wasn't looking. Took J.C. at his word. Why wouldn't she?"

"You know, I heard an NPR discussion on sociopaths. And J.C. had all the characteristics: manipulative, a flatterer. Discerned your weakness and zoomed in on it to take advantage of you. He perceived that Melanie was insecure about her looks and that was why he was always complimenting her about them. Melanie is the prettiest woman in Wilmington. When she's ninety, she'll be the prettiest woman in Wilmington. Still her strength is her weakness. She's insecure about her looks. I know that because I know her so well but few people do. And J.C. was canny enough to pick up on it.

"They say that one in twenty-five persons is a sociopath, no conscience, no guilt. They'll do anything to get what they want. J.C. was that one in twenty-five."

"There's just one thing that's bothering me. Why did he go after you? Why not Kelly? Or Babe?"

I shrugged. "We'll never know for sure, but Kelly had told him about the papers she'd removed to my house. Perhaps he thought that because I was experienced at analyzing old documents I might spot something that Kelly would overlook. And," I said grimly, "he might have had plans to take care of Kelly and Babe. Another brick tossed out of the second floor window at the house. A push down those basement steps would have done it."

"By why not remove the drawings and the albums from the house himself?" Jon persisted. "Destroy them."

"Ah. Kelly had the locks changed after Grandpa Joe died. She'd heard that thieves often rob a house while the family is at the funeral service. So she had solid locks installed on the doors and windows. And J.C. did not have a key; there was no reason to give him one. Grandpa Joe left the house to Kelly. J.C. had no interest in it."

"Okay," Jon said, "Meriweather's waiting. Let's get this over with. Are you sure you want to be there? If we're right, this will be grisly. You'd be better off waiting here in the car or on the porch."

"I want to come," I said and reached for the door handle. "I'll just sit on the steps."

Meriweather and three unformed officers plus Diane Sherwood greeted us and they looked as grim as I felt.

Willie Hudson had been summoned and he climbed down out of the cab of his truck and unloaded the tools we would need from the truck bed, then led the way into the house. He and Jon showed the police to the basement. I trailed after them, superfluous. After I had informed them of where to look, I wasn't needed.

I sat on the basement stairs and watched as they

dismantled the beautiful knotty pine tongue-and-groove paneling. Willie joined me on the steps. "I ain't got the stomach for this."

The sound of splintering wood was followed by a loud exclamation from one of the cops. "He's here!" he shouted. "What's left of the poor devil."

As I observed their excitement, I wondered how the family had not known that a man had been buried in their basement. Wouldn't there have been an odor? I asked myself. But the house was solid and the ceilings were high, and as Kelly had said there were fans in all the rooms so perhaps the odor had dissipated.

Then I recalled the humidor in the library and the fact that Joseph Lauder had loved cigars. The smell of his cigars had been a cover, I realized.

I was feeling queasy and decided to leave, to go outside and get some fresh air. But when I stood up, my head swam and the back of my shorts was wet. Had I been sitting in a wet spot? I wondered, and looked down at the step where I'd been sitting.

Before I could touch the wetness there, I saw blood pouring down my legs. No, oh no, I silently cried. Not that.

Willie was up and yelling for Jon. "Jon, over here! You cops! Get an ambulance!"

The police surrounded me and gently reclined

me onto the concrete floor. Diane Sherwood braced my head in her lap. Jon ripped off his shirt, wadded it in a ball and stuffed it between my legs in an attempt to staunch the flow of blood. Then the cramps began and I cried out.

Maybe it was because a police officer had called, or maybe it was because we were not far from the medical center, but within minutes I heard the unmistakable warbling of an ambulance.

The EMTs moved me onto a stretcher and ran with me up the stairs and out into the waiting ambulance where they started an IV line and clapped an oxygen mask over my face. Jon jumped into the ambulance with me. "I'm her husband," he said. "I'm going too."

A team of doctors and nurses met us on the sidewalk in front of the emergency room entrance. They ran alongside the stretcher, one of the nurses talking to me, trying to reassure me. But by then I had lost so much blood I was starting to fade.

Jon, shirtless, was trotting along too and one of the docs told him he couldn't come. "If you want to do something useful," he called over his shoulder as he ran, "go give blood."

The nurse held my hand. "Are you pregnant, honey?"

"Yes," I whispered. "I just found out."

"How far along."

"Two months, I think."

"Don't you worry none, honey, we're going to take good care of you, real good care of you." And then I passed out.

TWENTY-NINE

WHEN I AWOKE I thought I was in a sunlit rose garden. There were roses all around me and their fragrance filled the room. I realized it was morning for the sun was filtering through the windows. And the roses were in vases and set all around the room. I was in a hospital room, and in a flash I remembered everything that had happened until I passed out on the stretcher.

"Hey," Jon said softly and I turned my head to see him sitting next to the bed. "Welcome to the land of the living."

I started to cry, remembering everything. "I lost my baby, didn't I?" I sobbed. "Tell me the truth. I lost it."

"Yes," he said sadly. "Ashley, why didn't you tell me you were pregnant? Or confide in Melanie, someone?"

"I felt I had to tell Nick before I told anyone else, but…well, you know, I couldn't reach him."

Jon took my hand. "I would have taken better care of you if I had known."

"Tell me what happened? What day is it?"

"It's Thursday. You've been asleep since yesterday. The doctor said you needed to rest. You can discuss the medical stuff with her but this is what she told me." He got a shy look on his face. Jon is so transparent. It's always possible to tell what he is thinking.

"They think I'm your husband," he said shyly, "that's why they told me. Anyway, they had to do an emergency D and C. That stopped the bleeding and saved your life. You had a transfusion, two pints of O positive. I gave blood but I'm not your type. Melanie gave blood too. We all did in the Hematology Department."

"Is Melanie here?" I asked.

"Outside," he replied, "and having a fit. They'll only let us in one at a time. Your Aunt Ruby is outside too. And Binkie. Mickey left for Atlantic City this morning. I don't think he's coming back. Gordon Cushman went to the police and spilled everything, all about the illegal gambling ring Mickey was running." He smiled then. "And wait till you hear this. Binkie and Ruby are getting married. Isn't that cool?"

"Yes. Cool," I whispered, and in spite of feeling sorry for myself I was happy for them.

I wanted to ask the next question but couldn't bring myself to say the words.

Jon leaned closer to my bedside. "Ashley, don't be scared. They think everything is okay. She said you'll be able to get pregnant again and have babies." He took my hand. "So don't worry. God, I was so scared, if anything ever hap…"

A loud commotion outside my door interrupted his words. The door opened part way, someone was trying to come in, someone else was holding the door shut. I heard Nick's voice and he was yelling, "I'm her husband! You can't keep me out. Now let me go to her."

He entered my room in a rush and seemed to fill it, larger than life. Coming straight to my bed, he reached for me. "Sweetheart, sweetheart, I came right away as soon as I got word that your mother had died. I'm so sorry I wasn't here. I've been on airplanes for two days. They had me on special as-signment in Baghdad, but I got here as fast as I could."

"Why didn't you call me?" I said accusingly.

He looked sorrowful. "They wouldn't let me. I couldn't let anyone know where I was. Not even you."

"So you just left me to worry," I said softly as tears welled in my eyes.

The nurse, who was as bossy as all nurses are, had followed him into the room. "Well, if you're her husband, who is he?" she demanded, pointing to Jon.

Jon ducked his head and looked contrite.

When he didn't protest, she crossed her arms and said, "Well, one of you has got to go. Doctor's orders, one visitor at a time. You'll wear this poor girl out and she needs to get her strength back."

Nick looked confused. Jon my husband?

Jon sprang up, not doing a good job of controlling his fury. "I may not be her husband but I'm the one who brought her in! I'm the one who was here all night pacing the halls! If anyone stays, it's me."

Nick nodded. "Jon, you were good to help us out. Ashley and I appreciate what you did, but I'm here now so you can go home and get some well-deserved rest. Thanks, buddy, thanks a lot." He extended his hand but Jon did not take it, just glared at him.

"You should have been here for her," he declared. "She was worried to death over you, and I hold you responsible for what's happened to her."

I stared at the two of them, almost too overwhelmed to speak and certainly too weak. But I had to say my piece.

"Nick, I respect what you do, I really, really do. I understand that with you duty comes first. But with Jon, I come first. And Nick, when I do have a baby I want it to be with a man who puts *us* first. I'm sorry. I've been so lonely. I needed you so much."

"I wish I'd known," Nick said and the regret he felt was apparent.

"I tried to tell you as soon as I knew. I called and called." Tears rolled down my cheeks. "But now… there is no way I will ask Jon to leave this room."

Nick stared from Jon to me, instantly comprehending. Then, as if drawing a curtain between us, he let a mask of indifference slip over his face. He's assuming his cop's mode, I thought, and recalled how I had always resented the way he was able to hide his emotions behind a passive expression.

Nick moved to the door. "Okay, I'll wait outside. But we're going to talk about this later, Ashley."

Tears flooded my eyes. "I don't think so," I whispered as the door closed.

I stretched out my hand to Jon. "Please stay with me."

He grinned broadly and promised, "I'm not going anywhere."